Quartet  Qrime

HELL'S ANGEL

Also by Anthea Cohen

ANTHEA COHEN

Hell's Angel

QUARTET QRIME

First published by Quartet Books Limited 1986
A member of the Namara Group
27/29 Goodge Street, London W1P 1FD

Copyright © 1986 Anthea Cohen

British Library Cataloguing in Publication Data

Cohen, Anthea
Hell's angel.
I. Title
823'.914[F]   PR6053.O34/

ISBN 0 7043 2560 8

Typeset by MC Typeset, Chatham, Kent

Printed by Chanctonbury Press Ltd.
West Chiltington, Sussex.

1

The bright spring sunshine shone down on the great complex of Hemmington General Hospital, with its E-shaped buildings gleaming in the sunlight. Behind and around the hospital green fields and clusters of trees stretched away towards the undulating downs, throwing the modern buildings which were slightly raised above the surrounding countryside into greater relief.

In front of Hemmington General Hospital the many beautifully cut and tended lawns were divided by numerous paths with attendant blue and white signposts – some had arrows pointing to Pathological Laboratory, X-ray Department, Casualty, Out Patients, others a list of wards and their description: Gynaecological, Orthopaedic, Geriatric, Genito-urinary. A wide tarmac road between grass verges swept away to the left, going slightly downhill, bordered by young saplings at wide intervals. This road eventually joined the main road which linked the town and the many tiny, scattered surrounding villages served by the hospital. The population of these villages was at last becoming accustomed to the one large unit instead of the smaller town hospitals and several cottage hospitals to which they had been very attached in the past and which they had relinquished only after many heated meetings, protests and letters to the local papers.

This morning the front door of the hospital, which was at the end of the middle arm of the E, was spilling nurses, young doctors, porters, administrators, cleaners and secretaries into the brisk morning air. They were shouting and laughing and carrying placards, large pieces of cardboard nailed to sticks from the carpenters' workshop. On each piece of cardboard was written a slogan announcing the fact that they wanted more money, shorter hours and better conditions. It was a lively, and yet to some a depressing, almost horrifying sight.

A green double-decker bus, engine throbbing, was waiting to take them to Hemmington, the town that gave the hospital its name. The bus usually conveyed patients or visitors, and its use today had caused some controversy, but those who did not agree with this demonstration had been overruled.

The sight was particularly depressing to Sister Carmichael who stood in the hallway watching them pass, watching them jostle their way out through the big glass doors held open for them by two green-overalled workers who were shouting raucously: 'Come on, boys and girls, you've only got two hours. We want to let the people see us, don't we. Up the workers!'

Carmichael's lips curled in distaste as they responded equally loudly: 'Not 'alf, certainly we do, we don't want to waste any time. We'll tell them – we'll let them know what we want.'

The moment they got into the open air, the nurses among the crowd were dishevelled by the wind. Their cloaks blew about, their hair was whisked out from under their precariously pinned paper caps. To Carmichael the whole thing was degrading, especially for the nurses. She wished she had not bothered to come along to the hall to witness it. Her face must have expressed her feelings for a bearded administrator in neat grey suit, collar and tie, stopped in front of her, his expression belligerent.

'Don't look like that, Sister Carmichael, you'll be only too pleased to take whatever rise or shorter hours we get. I know your sort, you don't want to join in but you'll profit by it, anything we get, you'll profit by.'

Carmichael did not care to answer him and turned away. She was quite surprised that he knew her name, for in this huge hospital there was an anonymity unlike anything she had known before in the smaller hospitals where she had worked. In St Jude's and Greyfriars everyone had known everyone else, the sisters had been a little coterie of friends. It was not like that here, Carmichael thought. The sisters numbered scores, and as for the nurses, well you'd be lucky if you got anyone appointed to your department that you'd ever seen before, let alone knew.

The three telephonists had left their boards which were

buzzing with unattended calls in order to wave the strikers out. Two hours the demonstrators were going for, two hours to march the streets. Carmichael didn't know what the public would think, but she knew what her opinion was.

She turned away and walked back to her own department, the department that she was proud of yet had not wanted. A lot had happened to Carmichael in the last three years and most of it had been depressing.

At Greyfriars she had felt certain of getting a nursing officer's post. She hadn't realized that nowadays you had to be young, and young meant in your twenties, not in your late thirties. She had applied for a senior nursing officer's job, after Miss O'Donoghue had married and gone to Australia, but had not got the post. A twenty-seven-year-old from another hospital had been appointed. Having applied for another nursing officer's post and again having been turned down for a younger woman, Carmichael had decided in a fit of depression and rage that she must move on. She could not go on being sister of the orthopaedic ward, no matter how efficient and dedicated she was, for another ten, twelve or more years before she could retire. No, she thought with great reluctance, she must change her hospital, much as she loved Greyfriars she must leave it.

It had hurt her badly. She had grown so fond of the little hospital: it was just the size she liked, the number of beds she was used to. But then an advertisement for another nursing officer's post in this huge hospital, Hemmington General, had appeared in the *Nursing Mirror* and she had applied. Again a twenty-eight-year-old had got the job. By this time Carmichael realized that such a post was no longer available to her, so she had taken the next best thing, the post of senior sister in the large new Casualty department at Hemmington General.

When Carmichael had come for her interview and had first seen the department it had intimidated her, it was so different from the small, cosy Greyfriars Casualty department. Here there were two half circles of eight examination rooms, all curtained off, a large dressing station, a Casualty officer's office as well as beautifully appointed clinic rooms, toilets, recovery rooms, and three modern, well-equipped operating theatres. Her own office was carpeted, beautifully furnished, with a wash

3

basin, desk and chairs. She liked the way she was treated. Fresh flowers were put on her desk about every three days by the flower lady, a fact which both flattered and pleased her.

In the middle of the ring of examination rooms, clinic rooms and theatres was the nursing station where a nurse sat overseeing everything going on around her, even including the clerk's small office. She could answer patients' or relatives' queries and clear up any small problems for them, that is if they did not wish to see the sister of the department, the senior sister, Sister Carmichael. It was beautifully planned, but so sterile, so cold – not physically cold of course because the heating was always perfect, thermostatically controlled – but emotionally cold. Carmichael felt sometimes she was operating a large machine. However, the department was busy, the pay was good, everything about the job had prestige. She had a junior sister, four staff nurses, eight nurses in training, auxiliaries, and a clerk – although the clerk did not come under her jurisdiction. It was a large staff.

Carmichael squared her shoulders in the old familiar way as she walked back to the department. She always did this when she thought of her new post. She stood up straighter, held up her head. She'd come up, not down, that was what one had to do – go up – but the feeling haunted her that at forty-two she could go no further. It would be as much as she could do to keep at her present level until her pension arrived to free her from the whole scene. She would never have dreamed earlier that she could feel like this about nursing, have such thoughts, but it had come to that.

The recent past had much to do with it. Leaving her beloved little cottage in its leafy secluded lane, moving away from the vicinity of the charming rural town in which Greyfriars Hospital had been situated, selling her lovingly acquired furniture, abandoning her dear little garden, it had all been traumatic.

She missed her cats too. Two of them had died, but Tibbles was now housed with Mrs Jenks, an old friend who loved the cat as much as Carmichael did and whom Carmichael could trust, but the parting had been a great sadness, a wrench and, leaving Tibbles, Carmichael had been buoyed up only by the feeling that somehow one day she would get her back.

The nurses in this great hospital were well catered for. At the side of the hospital, lying well back from the road and surrounded by its own grounds, was a large, long building made up of flatlets. Each contained a bedroom, sitting room and bathroom, and shared a kitchen with three others. Carmichael found this adequate, but even so it made her homesick for her cottage, for her privacy and most of all for her garden.

When she came off duty, particularly in the evening, and closed her door behind her, she was lonely, lonelier, she felt, than she had been for years. In the cottage with her cats the feeling of loneliness had been kept at bay. There was not as much mixing of staff here as there was in a small hospital and, although Carmichael was well aware that her personality did not invite friendship, there was not even as much communication.

She often comforted herself by getting out her building society passbook and contemplating its total, made up of the money from the sale of her cottage and her savings. It was accumulating interest ready for the day when she could retire and buy another, similar cottage. The little blue building society book meant a lot to Carmichael. Looking at it never failed to appease her feeling of isolation, of loneliness. Now her greatest sense of fulfilment seemed to come when she visited the town and added to her savings. It was a poor substitute, she was aware, for her cottage, for her cats, for her home, but she was at least preparing for retirement. She would have another garden, another cat, and maybe a dog. The money was slowly gathering and would be ready when she needed it. She always closed the little book and caressed it with her palms before slipping it into its little plastic envelope – it was like a friend, very much like a friend and perhaps, she sometimes thought wryly, a little more reliable.

2

When Carmichael arrived back in the Casualty department everything was quiet although it was only eleven o'clock. Forewarned of the strike she had advised all dressing and plaster patients to come early, or not till the afternoon. There were three nurses in the department at the moment, the skeleton staff that the administration had insisted on – one staff nurse, one pupil nurse and one auxiliary.

As Carmichael walked in there was no sign of the staff nurse and the other two were leaning against the nursing station counter talking.

'Can't you find any work to do, nurse?' Carmichael's voice was cold and brisk, the sight she had just witnessed in the front hall had done nothing to improve her temper.

The pupil nurse, dark, slim and petite, turned startled large blue eyes on her sister and scurried away. The other, the auxiliary nurse, did not move, but continued to lean on the counter of the station and surveyed Carmichael, her jaws moving slowly. She was a gum chewer, a habit forbidden by Carmichael in the department.

'Where is staff nurse?' Carmichael asked.

'I think she's in the loo, Sister,' answered Nurse Pearson.

'I see. Please don't chew gum on duty, I've told you often enough. It's a disgusting habit.'

Nurse Pearson looked at her levelly, took the gum out of her mouth, rolled it between her thumb and forefinger and deliberately stuck it under the rim of the counter beside her.

Carmichael's face expressed even more disgust.

'And don't do that, that is equally revolting, just the kind of behaviour I would expect from you.'

She knew her hostility was disproportionate to the act, but she felt like that, unreasonably hostile.

'Well, Nurse Pearson, if you can't find anything else to do, I notice there is plaster on the bottom rungs of the operating table in theatre 3, perhaps you'll be good enough to clean it off.'

'I'm not a cleaner, Sister, that's not a nurse's job.' The auxiliary's rather over-made-up face flushed, and her lower lip stuck out. She was a bottle blonde, about thirty-eight Carmichael guessed. She had heard one of the porters call Nurse Pearson 'bedworthy'. According to rumours that description had often been tested.

'No, you're not a cleaner, but unfortunately the cleaner has seen fit to go on strike and walk out of the hospital so I'm afraid you'll have to do her work at least for the two hours she is away. This can hardly be called a normal working day.'

Carmichael was referring to a pamphlet which had been circulated to all the nurses telling them exactly what work was expected of them and what was not.

'I don't see why I should, I don't see why I should be a scab,' answered Nurse Pearson haughtily.

'A scab? Well I don't really know what that means but I'm afraid you'll have to do what I say or be reported.'

Their eyes met for a couple of seconds, then the grey eyes of the peroxided blonde nurse vanished behind green-shadowed eyelids and she walked out and along a short corridor. Carmichael heard her fling open the door of the cleaners' cupboard and she came back carrying a cloth. Carmichael was still not satisfied.

'I'm afraid you'll have to get a bucket and wash it off and you must put some disinfectant in it.'

The nurse looked as if she was going to refuse again, but then turned on her heel and went to fetch the bucket and disinfectant. Carmichael smiled with grim satisfaction and turned towards her own office, noting as she did so that Nurse Bellowes, her staff nurse, was back in the department and appeared to be busy which was what Carmichael approved of and wanted.

Once inside her office she sat down for a moment and gazed round her. Each time she entered her office she was pleased with it. She had been in the department for some time and she still had not got over the fact that they had made such an attractive room for the sister. The desk and a swivel chair for her, two chairs on the other side of the desk for patients if she had to interview them, or relatives. There was a small cupboard in the corner for her cloak, a wash basin with a mirror over it, flowers on the desk, a picture on the wall which she had been allowed to choose given by the Friends of the hospital. Carmichael had chosen a Utrillo, a street scene, lonely and almost colourless. She'd chosen it because once, on a lonely holiday in London, she had come across it in an art gallery and for some reason never forgot the melancholy little painting.

She got up suddenly, feeling the wish to walk around her domain while she had time, while there were so few nurses and patients about.

First she went into the doctor's office. This was much the same as her own: a swivel chair, a desk, chairs opposite, and a similar cupboard in the corner. Carmichael wished there were more women doctors, she might have made a friend of one, someone easy to talk to, easier that is . . . Carmichael did not find men easy to talk to except of course Harry. She brushed him from her mind hastily.

The Casualty doctor, Dr Singh, was pleasant but he talked more to her junior nurses than to her. They often surprised her by knowing so much about him – that he was going out with an English girl, what her name was, what she was like – because he told Carmichael nothing. When he was off duty Casualty was covered by a junior Casualty officer who in Carmichael's opinion was little more than a boy. She felt she had to keep a very stern eye on him. When both of these were off duty, and when they were very busy, the job was done, usually reluctantly, by the house officers, who had to be torn away from their own duties. The one woman house officer was, Carmichael thought, a feeble creature, who was much too friendly with the junior nurses and of course the junior doctors.

The Casualty department was the responsibility of the senior orthopaedic surgeon. Carmichael did not get on particularly well with him. He was retiring this week and had stayed on a little longer until they found a successor for him. Carmichael felt that he did not give the attention to Casualty that it really warranted. However, she would know soon, probably this week, who his successor was to be. She hoped he would be more interested in Casualty and perhaps insist on one more Casualty officer to be added to the establishment. It was needed. She longed to show how efficient she was. She was glad she had had some time to get used to the place and the department. It was a busy Casualty and as if echoing her thoughts at that moment she heard the sound of a siren approaching the ambulance area.

The little dark nurse looked up alertly and put her head out of the dressing room where Carmichael had seen her tucking a sheet in place on the couch inside. As she came out her eyes met Sister Carmichael's.

'Shall I have to take particulars while the clerk's away, Sister?' she asked.

Carmichael nodded. She liked this nurse. She was pretty but more malleable than the blonde woman who now came in having thrown the bucket and cloth back into the cleaner's cupboard and closed the door with a bang. Carmichael had heard her.

'Thank goodness something's coming in, at least I won't have to clean any more,' she said to Staff Nurse Bellowes, obviously for Carmichael's benefit, and hurried off into the ambulance entrance to meet the ambulance men, something with which Carmichael did not agree but which for the moment she ignored. Things were a little at sixes and sevens this morning and she would let it pass, but when her nurses came back she would show her disapproval by making them work harder and finding fault with everything they did. It was gratifying, she thought, to have the power to do so.

As the blonde nurse walked away, Carmichael noticed that a strand of hair had fallen down on to her collar.

'Nurse Pearson,' she called.

'The woman turned round, her grey eyes still hostile and resentful.

'Yes, Sister Carmichael,' she said.

'Your hair is falling down, it's most untidy, please go and put it up.'

The nurse put her hand hastily behind her neck, felt the strands that had fallen down and twisted them up angrily, took a pin from the usually neat coil at the back of her head and plunged it in.

'I bet she wishes hers could fall down like that,' she muttered to the staff nurse walking beside her. Perhaps she did not intend her superior to hear this but unfortunately Carmichael did hear.

'I will speak to you in my office after we've dealt with this casualty, Nurse Pearson,' said Carmichael coldly, but not before she had selfconsciously put up her hand to the closely cut hair at the back of her neck. It was true her fine, sandy hair was always tidy, there was hardly enough of it to be otherwise. She felt a quick flash of hatred towards the insolent woman. She knew just how the ambulance men would greet Nurse Pearson, with familiarity and yet liking. She knew the phrases they would use:

'How's your sex life, ducks, getting enough of it are we?' She knew too that Pearson would simper and bridle and give them back as good as they gave.

At that moment a ring came at the Casualty waiting-room door. A woman stood there holding by the hand a small, bawling child, his finger wrapped in a piece of rag.

'He shut his finger in his fire engine,' said the woman, her voice agitated. 'It looks as if it's squashed quite a bit or I wouldn't have brought him . . .'

This was not the ambulance patient, who was already being wheeled through the door at the side which admitted ambulance cases. Well, two patients would keep them busier, thought Carmichael, and that was satisfactory.

'Nurse,' she called to the dark-haired girl who came forward quickly. 'Take this lady's name and address and particulars please.'

The nurse walked into the clerk's office and the mother led the little child still crying after her.

'Name?' said the pupil nurse.

'Do you mean my name or . . .?'

The dark-haired girl pointed to the child.

'Bobby Banks,' said the woman, at the same time trying to hush the child.

The ambulance man spoke jovially to the blonde auxiliary nurse, as Carmichael had known he would.

'Nice young man for you, nurse, looks just your type,' he said jokingly. Then he saw Sister Carmichael and altered his tone hastily. 'A broken arm, Sister, may we bring him in?'

'Yes,' said Carmichael. She was glad that the two hours of the strike were not going to be empty of work. It would do them good to see that Casualty had been busy while they were away, indeed she would not have minded if the department had been stretched to breaking point. She beckoned the ambulance man imperiously, walked ahead of him and held aside one of the curtains so that they could back the trolley into the examination room. She took one look at the young man lying on the trolley, who was gazing inquiringly about him as he was pushed forward. He was a good-looking young man. She waved Nurse Pearson away, she would deal with this herself. She followed the trolley into the examination room and drew the curtains, noting with satisfaction the petulant look of frustration on Nurse Pearson's face. Anything in trousers, Carmichael thought. The curtain was drawn back again and for a moment Carmichael thought it was Nurse Pearson. It was Staff Nurse Bellowes. As she pulled the curtain aside she came through and pulled it closed after her.

'Can I relieve you, Sister?' she asked and Carmichael motioned her to do so. Staff Nurse Bellowes was neither young nor attractive, she would do nicely for this good-looking patient, Carmichael thought, and walked out of the examination room to telephone whichever Casualty officer was currently on duty. They would probably be sitting in the doctors' duty room looking vacantly at the television or reading the paper. Carmichael was not sorry to disturb them there. She was not sure who was on duty, as she did not know if any of the Casualty officers had been with the demonstrators.

The demonstrators returned to the hospital and to their various wards and departments. Carmichael could hear them clattering along still talking excitedly. She did not ask any of her striking staff how they had got on. They too were chatting among themselves, but the conversation ceased when she came near. The clerk resumed her duties with one or two sideways

11

glances at Sister Carmichael but said nothing, and Carmichael kept a grim silence for the rest of the day, nodding briefly when the nurses came up to ask to be excused to go to meals. She intended to show her disapproval of the whole thing and succeeded in doing so very well.

After lunch she called Auxiliary Nurse Pearson into her office. She did not ask her to sit down.

'Nurse Pearson,' she said, not looking at the girl but appearing to be examining some procedure notes. 'I do not find your work particularly satisfactory. I have noticed one or two things, and given you some instructions you have not complied with. I don't know if it is that you dislike Casualty. Perhaps you would like to be moved back to a ward?'

'I like it all right. It's as good as anywhere else.' Nurse Pearson looked at Carmichael sullenly.

'That's hardly the right attitude, you have to like where you work, show a little more enthusiasm about it.'

'No have to about it. I just do the work and go off – and forget about it.'

'Yes, so it seems,' said Carmichael. 'Hardly vocational.'

'Oh come on, Sister, vocational, well it's a word you don't use now, it's out of date, it's from way back, Florence Nightingale and all that really. It's just a job, isn't it? I don't grumble about it, I don't grumble about the hours or anything, I just do it. I think the hours are too long and the pay is too low, that's why I agreed with the strike and I'd have gone if you'd have let me. But it's only a job. Vocational!'

Carmichael felt a sudden depression. She looked up at the woman standing in front of her, plump, sexy, sure of herself, insolent, and Carmichael sensed she was strong, strong in the belief that she was right. Carmichael suppressed a sigh.

'Very well, Nurse Pearson. If that's how you feel about the job perhaps I can understand your attitude a little more, but I'm afraid I don't approve of it and it's you who will have to change, not me.'

'All right then, I'll do my best,' said Nurse Pearson, turning on her heel with a familiar twitch of her bottom. She walked out and Carmichael could not help feeling that Pearson, not she, the sister of the department, had had the last word.

3

At the end of a day which, as the afternoon had drawn on, had been pretty busy Carmichael went into her office. She was about to change her shoes when there was a knock on the door. She called out, 'Just a moment,' slipped her feet into her mufti shoes, put her duty shoes in her cupboard and opened the door.

It was Miss Haskins, the young house officer whom Carmichael rather despised. She wore glasses that were apt to slip to the end of her usually greasy nose and was a timid, but fairly efficient girl.

'May I come in? Oh, sorry.' Miss Haskins always seemed to be apologizing.

Carmichael opened the door wider and waved her in.

'Yes, yes, it's all right, do come in. I was just getting ready to go home. Do you want me?' she asked. She wanted to get up to the changing room and then over to the home to try and banish this rather disagreeable day from her thoughts, but she managed a wintry smile for Miss Haskins.

'Oh, it's just a bit of news I thought you might like to hear,' said Miss Haskins and her eyes, rather pink-rimmed behind her glasses as though she had been up all night, which indeed she often was, blinked at Carmichael short-sightedly.

'It's the new orthopaedic surgeon, I've found out his name. He comes tomorrow. I don't know if he's going to start work immediately but he definitely comes, he definitely arrives tomorrow.'

She said this with a certain triumph and relish and Carmichael wondered if perhaps she was interested in knowing what kind of man he was and if he was married. Everyone in hospital seems anxious to get married, Carmichael thought again with contempt. She was sure that with some of the nurses that's what they came for, to catch a doctor, or any man come to that.

'Oh, what's his name then? Who is he and where does he come from, what hospital I mean?' Carmichael's interest was not altogether feigned, she really wanted to know. It was important that the man, who in a way would be her boss, and who would expect the department to be run the way he liked it, should be someone she could get on with. She was quite as anxious to know about him as this timid little house officer.

The doctor looked at her and smiled, her hands deep in the pockets of her white coat, obviously enjoying the fact that she had news to impart.

'It's a man named Nigel Denton,' she said. 'I don't know what other posts he's held, but he's done a lot of casualty they say as well as orthopaedic work. I believe he's from George's, they say he's quite good, particularly on hips, it's his speciality they say.'

Nigel Denton. The name meant quite a lot to Carmichael. It must be the same man, the name was not a common one. And if it was, she had known him way back. She had known him at St Jude's, the first hospital in which she had been staff nurse. He was a nice man, but, if she remembered rightly he had had a drink problem then. Her memory flashed back to a night in Casualty when she had worked with him and then had been told off for being there. She remembered a lot of things in that instant as she stood there silently.

Getting no answer, the house officer touched Carmichael's arm.

'You were miles away then, Sister Carmichael. Do you know him, do you know Mr Denton?'

'I think I may have met him,' said Sister Carmichael. She was always guarded about anything in her past. 'Yes, I think I may have met him in a hospital I worked in.'

'Oh well, that will be pleasant if you're old friends, that will be great, you can talk about old times and that always . . .'

'I did not say we were old friends, I said I had met him him in a hospital I had worked in. If you don't mind, Miss Haskins, I'd like to . . .'

Miss Haskins immediately shrank into herself as she always did even if only mildly rebuffed.

'Oh yes, yes, of course. I'm so sorry. I just came down to Casualty to see that foreign body in eye that nurse rang me about. I'm sorry, I didn't mean to hold you up.'

Carmichael relented a little.

'That's all right, it was nice of you to tell me. You say he's coming tomorrow? Well, I suppose that will be something to look forward to, won't it?'

Miss Haskins nodded and scurried out.

Carmichael smiled a little grimly. She looked round her office to see that all was tidy. The report book was on her desk. She closed it and picked it up. Her junior sister was off today. She suddenly thought of her with a pang of disquiet. Nurse Taylor was young and pretty, divorced, but that didn't make any difference these days and Nigel Denton well . . . She tried to remember about his wife . . . but of course she was dead, he'd killed her, hadn't he, in a car accident? But perhaps he'd married again.

Abstractedly Carmichael carried the book over to the nursing station and placed it ready for the staff nurse to read through; all the admissions into Casualty for that day, all those who had been admitted to the wards, and all those who had been sent home, every detail punctiliously filled in by Carmichael.

'I'm off now, staff nurse,' she said and the staff nurse came forward, saw the book on the nursing station and smiled at Carmichael.

'Thank you, Sister. Miss Haskins is just looking at that foreign body in eye, I don't think it's very serious though.'

'I know,' said Carmichael and walked out of the department. As she did so she heard another ambulance wailing as it went into the ambulance bay. She made her way briskly to the changing room and, having changed, came down, walked through the front door and made her way across the wide area of beautifully kept lawns and gravel paths. She always appreciated the way they were cut and edged and kept so well.

The nurses' home lay fairly close to the hospital, across what was the main hospital road and then down a black, tarmac path, wide enough for two cars to pass. It was bordered on each side

15

with flowerbeds.

She looked with appreciation at the spring wallflowers blowing gently in the borders. As she walked by she breathed in their scent, and for some reason thought of their other name – gilly flowers. Then she looked back at the gleaming new hospital. It was nice to work there, in spite of the fact that it was so impersonal. If ever she wanted to leave it would be good to be able to say that she had been there in a responsible position. But what sort of post would she get from here? No, she might well have to stay, she saw at the moment no point in moving on, but then she had only been here a short time. It would suffice to stay here for quite . . . It would be like moving in a straight line instead of upwards if she left here, or even in a downward line and that would not do.

A nurse smiled at her as she passed.

'Hallo, Sister Carmichael. Don't the flowers smell nice?'

She had gone past before Carmichael had time to reply. It was a young, rather pert nurse who had worked in her department some time ago, but strangely enough Carmichael had rather liked her and was now pleased that she had spoken to her and remembered her. She raised a hand and smiled but did not answer. Even now her thoughts were elsewhere.

She walked on and entered the door of the nurses' home, an equally bright, equally new and equally impersonal building. As she entered she was aware that her head ached. Tension, she thought, that beastly strike and what good would it do? All their shouting and walking through the streets just lowered them in the eyes of the public, damaged their cause rather than did it any good. Carmichael felt that nurses should never demonstrate, and neither should doctors. Whatever cleaners and porters and the administrative staff did was their business, but nursing and medicine were professions, professions that people should look up to, indeed be made to look up to because of the way their members behaved. The sight that must be presented by that motley crowd that she had witnessed going out of the hall this morning, well . . . No wonder, Carmichael thought, she had a headache.

4

The heavy glass doors of the nurses' home swung to behind Carmichael and the pleasant air-conditioned atmosphere immediately soothed her aching temples. Lately, anything disturbing, such as today's withdrawal of labour or the unpleasant behaviour of her auxiliary nurse, was enough to give Carmichael a headache which was sometimes so bad she could hardly see. She now knew why the patients sometimes spoke of their blinding headaches, although formerly she had suspected them of exaggeration.

She decided to take two pain-relieving tablets and lie on the bed till the throbbing in her head had subsided before making up her mind whether to cook herself some supper or go over to the nurses' dining room in the hospital.

From the bathroom cabinet she took a packet of tablets, tore the gold cover from two of them and swallowed them with the aid of a glass of water. Then she stretched herself out on her bed and closed her eyes.

Behind her closed eyelids a procession of people and events began to pass, people and events she felt were to blame for her present condition: Marion Hughes, Margaret Tarrant, Emily Maitland, Harry Maitland. They had all contributed to her breakdown and were responsible for the fact – though she could not at the moment think how – that she had not got the promotion she deserved.

Now here was Nigel Denton coming back into her life like the fragment of an old memory. He, personally, had done nothing to hurt her, but – would he remember her? She doubted it. People didn't remember her. She was a nonentity. The old familiar dark depression threatened to cover her head like a cloud. No matter how familiar it was, it was still terrifying. To wake again each morning as she had once done in the same endless tunnel of darkness, feeling: what's the use? What's it all for? Why try? Why do anything? She couldn't bear that again. She remembered her terrible plunge into the river, the cold water, the taste of pollution. She felt that if the same cloud came back, the same tunnel, she would wish, as she did sometimes even now, that everything had ended there in the river.

Abruptly she rose from the bed though her head was still thumping. If she allowed herself to go on thinking like this she would not drop off to sleep, the tablets would not work. It would be better to be occupied than lying here thinking – that might bring on a return of the dreaded depression that had put her into a psychiatric ward and was still one of her greatest fears.

She would go and see if there was any post for her. Carmichael received very few letters but she had recently sent for a 'conditioning hairbrush', that promised to thicken and wave her hair. She did not believe the claims, she had tried remedies for her scanty, fine, sandy-coloured hair too often without success, but the brush was inexpensive and she had thought that perhaps it might do something for her.

In the pigeon-hole marked 'C' in the hall though there was no packet, there was a letter and it was for her. It was from Jones, her friend at St Matthew's Hospital, the sister of the children's ward. She recognized the writing and was surprised because Jones had written only two weeks ago and Carmichael had not yet replied to that letter. She walked slowly back to her room, slitting the top of the letter with her thumbnail as she did so.

Back in her room she sat down in her comfortable armchair to read the letter, rubbing her left temple with her forefinger. She felt the vein under the tip of her finger, hurting, tender. The letter began: 'Dear Agnes, Great news.'

Carmichael could hardly believe what she read. Jones, fat, amiable, waddling, not terribly efficient Jones had been promoted to nursing officer. It was a stunning blow for Carmichael, and, coupled with her pumping headache, made her feel sick; that Jones should be a nursing officer while she

18

herself was still just a sister and likely to remain so. The letter continued in a triumphant strain and ended: 'I expect you'll be surprised to hear of my good luck, but I wanted you to be the first to know.'

For a long time Carmichael looked blankly out of the window. The light was fading on the pleasant view of trees and lawns and flowerbeds. Twilight was gradually turning to darkness. Carmichael sat still, automatically stroking her aching temple. To the right lay a shrubbery which was still vaguely visible in outline. Behind it was a teak seat, new and shiny with varnish where Carmichael sometimes took a book and sat in seclusion. Now she just gazed and gazed, not registering anything that her eyes saw, thinking of the letter that lay in her lap.

At last she got up, closed the window and switched on her bedside lamp. The tablets had done nothing to ease her headache. She read the letter again. How could this have happened to Jones? How? She was not particularly efficient and she was at least thirty-eight – quite that. Carmichael went into her tiny bathroom and ran cold water on to her face flannel. She went back and sat down again and placed the cold, wet flannel over her eyes, pressing its ends against her temples. For some time there was no noise in the home to disturb her and after a while the stabbing pains in her head decreased. She tried to put everything away from her, stop thinking, but it was not easy. At last she fell into an uneasy doze and then woke up, stifled. She removed the face flannel, now almost dry.

As she opened her damp lids and gazed out of the window into the darkness, a pair of eyes met hers from the other side of the glass, wide, wild and bloodshot, set in a round, red face which was pressed against the window, distorting the shape of the nose. The face was clean-shaven and shiny and surrounded by spiky black hair.

Carmichael stood up abruptly and the man retreated away from the window, stepping back across the path to the lawn. As he did so he held open his big, black overcoat and the light from the bedside lamp shining through the window showed that he was stark naked.

Carmichael crossed the room and hastily pulled the curtains.

19

She heard the man's footsteps running away along the tarmac path. Disgusted more than alarmed, she left her room and made her way to the hall and dialled the hospital. The electric clock above the telephone showed that it was 9.20. As she stood there with the phone in her hand a nurse came through the front door. She stopped dialling for a moment and turned and said: 'Did you see anyone outside?'

The nurse shook her head. She was young and pretty and unknown to Carmichael. She looked at her curiously.

'Why, something up?' she asked.

'A Peeping Tom,' said Carmichael, not elaborating further.

The young nurse grimaced.

'Oh, good Lord, not another! I'm glad I didn't bump into him.'

It was not until she was out of earshot that Carmichael told the full story to the night superintendent. He said immediately that he would get in touch with the police and went on: 'And I'd better ring up Mr Stewart, too. After all, he is hospital secretary. He might like to get the police himself or tell me to. You know how he is. Do you think the chap is still around?'

Carmichael said that she had heard him run away and put the telephone down.

She suddenly realized as she made her way back to her room that her headache was better and that she felt slightly hungry. She decided to go into the kitchen and heat some milk. The one thing she disliked about the arrangements in the nurses' home was sharing the kitchen. She disliked going there in her dressing-gown to make herself a late-night drink. She sometimes met a junior nurse there and she felt that her dressing-gown and slippers did nothing to increase her dignity, and thought too that personal involvement with junior nurses was unwise. She had suggested several times that the senior nursing staff should have a kitchen of their own.

This time, however, not a junior nurse but a sister whom Carmichael vaguely recognized was in the kitchen, and as Carmichael entered she looked up.

'Hallo. Carmichael, isn't it?'

'Yes,' Carmichael answered with her usual reserve. The woman was fat and friendly with a mop of unruly hair almost to her shoulders. Most unsuitable for anyone of that age, thought Carmichael with automatic disapproval. This sister looked at least fifty and her purple dressing-gown hung open revealing a flowered nightdress.

'Sister O'Hara,' she said, smiling broadly and showing excellent white teeth. 'Having an early night. Want an egg?' she went on and pointed to a box of six on the table. 'A patient's visitor brought them for me, decent of him, he's a farmer, they're free range. Go on, have one.'

Carmichael hesitated.

'Worried about the cholesterol?' O'Hara said, seeing Carmichael's hesitation.

'Not at all, I'd like one, thank you. May I put it in with yours?'

'Casualty aren't you?' O'Hara asked and without waiting for an answer continued, 'I'm men's surgical, well genito-urinary, the water babies, dear old chaps.'

'Yes, I'm the Casualty sister, the senior Casualty sister,' said Carmichael.

The other woman's frank, big-busted sensuality made Carmichael as usual feel slightly uncomfortable. She was glad when O'Hara spooned the eggs out of the boiling water and handed one to Carmichael in an egg-cup. Carmichael thanked her and O'Hara gave her a warm smile and lifted a hand in farewell. As she did so Carmichael noticed the glint of a gold wedding ring and was glad she had not mentioned the naked man. She was not sure why. Perhaps a vague feeling that this woman would only laugh about it and say: 'Poor chap must want something to do,' or something like that.

As these thoughts went through her mind Carmichael was conscious of a return of the depression that the incident with the flasher and the brief contact with O'Hara had temporarily dispelled.

Back in her room she ate the egg with more enjoyment than she expected and finished with an apple. She put the tray on the table to be dealt with later.

She was about to get ready for bed when she realized that she would probably have to speak to the police when they came, if they came. She summoned up again the picture of the naked man with his red face and round eyes. Suddenly, for some reason that she could not place, she felt curiously elated and decided that while she was waiting she would go back to the kitchen and make herself some hot milk. She went along carrying the tray, switched on the light in the now empty kitchen, and realized that she was smiling and that her headache had completely gone.

Carmichael could never quite understand her own feelings. She recognized them, but made no attempt to analyse them. She could no longer expect ever to do so, she thought. She accepted her reactions, accepted the fact that a crisis of feelings did not always fill her with dread or fear, but sometimes with a vague excitement.

The police did arrive and searched the grounds round the nurses' home. It was no difficult task for the young trees so lately planted gave little chance of concealment. Only the shrubbery was a possible lurking place and that took only seconds to search.

Carmichael described the man precisely to them and earned a compliment from the grey-haired sergeant. After suggesting that all the nurses in the home should lock their windows that night, they left. Carmichael disliked sleeping with her windows closed: being on the ground floor, she decided, had its disadvantages. There were only two floors, but Carmichael had chosen a downstairs flat because they were the only ones with bathrooms *en suite*. These had been built for senior staff and Carmichael felt that she deserved senior quarters.

She prepared for bed. It was not until she had switched out her lights and had her head on the pillow that the news about Jones came back to her, but this time it was not quite so . . . nursing officer . . . but after all St Matthew's was a tiny hospital, not like this one. Being a sister here was a responsible and important job. She must invite Jones for a visit. There was a guest room in the nurses' home, all mod. cons. She would show her round this huge hospital. Her large casualty department. It would be pleasant and she felt better about her friend's promotion, better able to accept the fact that Jones was now senior to her. She would show her this place and that would make her think . . . on this happy note she fell deeply asleep.

It was 3 a.m. by her little bedside clock when something woke her. She sat bolt upright in bed, a dream of the naked man slowly clearing from her memory. The sound of laughter and voices passed outside her door – nurses returning from a party. She frowned. What a time to come in. Did they expect to be really alert tomorrow while they were on duty. Disgraceful. She frowned there in the darkness and thought for some reason of O'Hara . . . bedworthy . . . again that word. How she hated it. Carmichael lay down again but this time it took her longer to fall asleep.

5

Next morning Carmichael went on duty. The few people she met at breakfast and on her way to the department did not mention the previous night's incident. In a small hospital like Greyfriars or St Matthew's or St Jude's it would have been the talk of the dining room. Everybody would have been surmising and excited and chatting. But here, because the hospital and the nurses' home were so big and contained so many people, nothing was said and Carmichael did not venture to refer to the incident.

However, when she got to her own department promptly at 8.30, one of her staff nurses did come forward immediately and say: 'I hear you had a nasty thing happen last night, Sister Carmichael. It must have been horrible from what I hear.'

Carmichael looked at her and nodded, keeping the composure of which she was so proud and which, she felt, accorded with her experience and status and was so useful in keeping order in this large department where the sister must never be ruffled.

'Yes, indeed,' she said.

'Well, I hope they catch him, we don't want that kind of man wandering round the nurses' home, do we?'

Her junior sister, Sister Taylor, joined the two of them.

'No, I've never met a flasher and I don't want to. I think it's disgusting,' she said.

Carmichael looked at her just as coolly. 'Well, I expect the poor creature is deranged. He wouldn't behave like that if he weren't.'

'Oh, I dunno,' said Sister Taylor. 'Some men get a kick out of it. What did he look like?' The implication was obvious and the

24

staff nurse giggled.

'I really have no idea. I saw his face but little else,' said Carmichael. There was no room for laughter over the incident in her mind, though the other two looked at each other with meaning smiles. At that moment Carmichael noticed that the blonde, insolent auxiliary nurse was standing near by with a companion. Carmichael turned on her abruptly.

'You seem to have a genius, Nurse Pearson, for standing about doing nothing,' she said.

The woman tossed her head.

'I was doing something, I was going round getting the dressing rooms ready.'

'Well, you don't appear to be at the moment. You are just standing completely still,' said Carmichael, walking away to her office. As she did so she heard the blonde nurse whisper to the little dark nurse who was usually beside her – those two must be split up, they aren't good for each other, she thought automatically – 'Probably the first naked man she's seen for years, at least one that wasn't a patient.' They both laughed and Carmichael felt the colour rise to her cheeks, but she did not hesitate in her swift, prim walk towards her office.

Right, Nurse Pearson she said to herself grimly, your report won't be a good one when you leave here. I shall see to that.

She went into her office, picked up the report book which showed her how many admissions had been made through Casualty or treated in Casualty during the night and picked up a pen to sign it. So viciously did she use the pen that it almost went through the paper. The action boded ill for Auxiliary Nurse Pearson.

Mr Nigel Denton arrived in Casualty, accompanied by the retiring orthopaedic surgeon, Mr Wainwright, at about 11.30, when the department was in full swing. Nurses were bustling to and fro superintended by Sister Taylor and Sister Carmichael. As he walked into the department Carmichael's heart missed a beat, not because she admired Mr Denton particularly but because he was something from her past, and she wondered if he would remember her. As the two approached, Mr Wainright pointed this way and that explaining the positions of the operating theatres and the examination rooms. When he led Mr

Denton forward to meet Carmichael she realized he must have been to the hospital before for his interview, but she had not seen him then, and now she wondered if he would . . .she hoped very much for recognition.

Nigel Denton had changed, aged a little and Carmichael noticed grey hairs at the side of his head that were not there before. There were creases round his eyes and he had grown fatter, thicker in the waist. Thinking of the lurid stories she had heard about him at St Jude's, Carmichael wondered again if he still drank. Recollections of his wife and of the accident came to her mind, but what would come to his? Would he remember? She suddenly realized that no memories of her were coming to him because he looked at her quite blankly. Only when Mr Wainright mentioned her name did his face light up a little.

'This is Sister Carmichael, our Casualty sister, our senior Casualty sister, Mr Denton.'

'Why yes, I remember you in . . .where was it now?'

Carmichael held out her hand to shake his although he had not put his forward. He did then, however, and they clasped hands.Carmichael for some reason desperately wanted warmth. She smiled wanly and said; 'Yes, indeed we have met before, Mr Denton. It was at St Jude's. We must talk about it sometime, it would be nice . . .' Then, overcome by shyness, she turned on her heel and made her way towards the doctors' office. As she did so Sister Taylor came out of the dressing room, a plastic apron over her dress, her face slightly flushed. They had had a man in who had cut through the flex of his garden mower and electrocuted himself. He had been in violent spasm when he came in but was now quiet. Two young house officers were with him waiting for him to be admitted. Carmichael saw the quick look of admiration that crossed Denton's face as he looked at Sister Taylor and she felt the old, familiar bitterness. Looks were everything, she thought, and quite ridiculously wondered if the post this morning had brought the famous hairbrush to improve her hair.

Mr Wainwright introduced Sister Taylor to Nigel Denton, in Carmichael's opinion quite unnecessarily. She felt it was her job to introduce the junior staff, at least the staff nurses and her junior sister. She watched as the two faced each other.

26

'Busy department, Madeleine?' asked Denton smiling quizzically.

It was a nasty jolt for Carmichael. They knew each other, were on Christian name terms. For some reason Carmichael was filled with dismay.

'Busy enough, Nigel,' answered Madeleine Taylor, flushing even pinker. 'It keeps us on the go. Nice though. There's a factory near here, several accidents come from there, people are careless at work, aren't they?'

'Oh, you two know each other,' said Mr Wainwright.

Nigel Denton nodded, his eyes still on Madeleine Taylor's face.

'Yes, we have met,' he said, smiling broadly.

'We get quite a few fractured hips, it's an ageing population, well loaded with oldsters. Too many for Mr Wainright's beds sometimes,' Sister Taylor went on, glancing towards the senior orthopaedic surgeon and receiving a smile back.

During this conversation which almost excluded her, Carmichael's dismay increased. Some relationship between the consultant and her junior sister was obvious, yet why should she be so surprised? Was it a coincidence? Maybe, but she felt that they were more than acquaintances, and the anger and the tension came back as another thought crossed her mind. Was it a coincidence that Nigel Denton had sought this post, or was it because Madeleine Taylor was here? Unlikely, surely. Or had Taylor come to this hospital because Nigel Denton had told her of his intention to apply for the consultancy? Well, she would soon know and she would also try to arrange Sister Taylor's off-duty times so that their meetings would be less frequent. That at least she could do.

Mr Wainwright looked very pleased with himself, positively purring, thought Carmichael. Perhaps he was glad to be getting rid of the Casualty department which had never been a love of his. Carmichael hoped that under Nigel Denton's consultancy cover would perhaps improve. He might even be able to improve the doctor attendance, even wangle another Casualty officer – the place was busy enough to justify one.

In the doctors' office the two men sat down obviously wishing to talk together. Carmichael asked politely if they would like coffee. The orthopaedic surgeon said yes, in spite of the fact that Nigel Denton had shaken his head. However, Carmichael took it that they would both have some. As she walked away she remembered how once when Nigel Denton had been having coffee in Casualty and she had been there helping after an accident, he had put a dash of whisky in his cup from a flask in his pocket, winking at her as he did so. He had not worried then if he smelled of drink and she wondered if he was going to be the same here. She hoped devoutly that he had changed.

She left them, went back to her own office and telephoned to order coffee. The person at the other end in the kitchen queried the name.

'Denton? Who is he. A visitor or a relative or something?'

'He's the new orthopaedic surgeon and he would like the coffee at once. He's with Mr Wainwright so please get it down here immediately and see that it's hot.' Carmichael put the phone down but not before she had heard the kitchen worker say: 'Hoity-toity, then!'

There is no discipline, thought Carmichael, no discipline at all. It might be a big, new hospital but they had no idea how to keep people in their place. That was one of the things at which she felt she was good, but whether it was appreciated or not was doubtful. She thought of Jones, of how she would act, how she would keep discipline, she always wanted to be popular. Nursing officer! With her fat, round face and untidy hair! Well, she'd be popular, Carmichael supposed and that nowadays was everything. She slammed the book shut and went out to look critically into the dressing rooms where her staff were treating patients. As she did so the nurses stiffened and looked towards her with apprehension, some with forceps clutched in their plastic-gloved hands doing dressings which they knew she would criticize if there was the slightest thing wrong. Their looks of apprehension pleased Carmichael and she continued her round of the department, stopping at the clerk's office to tell her that her white coat was too short and showed too much of her legs.

The clerk, mutinous, looked at her and said: 'Well, I can't help it, I expect it's shrunk.'

Carmichael bent forward and picked up the end of the girl's

28

white coat.

'It's not shrunk at all, you've shortened it and shortened it very badly. You're not supposed to do that, you know, it's hospital property.'

'You're not in charge of me, Sister, you know that. I come under . . .'

'You're in my department and while you're here you'll look decent at least,' she said,turning on her heel and walking off to continue her inspection.

6

For the rest of the day Carmichael was acutely aware that Nigel Denton was around the hospital. She waited for him to come and talk to her. She expected to have a long session with him and was even more meticulous than usual with the running of the department, particularly in the morning when the two men were talking in the office over their coffee. She hoped to see him again so that he would make some remark about how well and efficiently the Casualty department appeared to be running.

The doctors stayed in the office for some time. They obviously had much to discuss and Carmichael was only too aware of this, but she felt selfconscious. She would be glad when a working relationship had been established between Mr Denton and herself. Then he would realize how efficient, how well run her Casualty department was. She was sure that Mr Wainwright would have little to complain of, but, knowing him, she did not feel he would be particularly enthusiastic as far as she was concerned because they had never struck up a really close relationship regarding the department. Well,not as close as Carmichael would have liked.

Meanwhile the usual string of cases came in. A small child who had swallowed a coin was dealt with by the Casualty officer, Dr Singh, carefully watched by Carmichael. The coin was extracted and the child left the department with her mother. There had been some crying, of course. That could not be avoided, but Carmichael bustled about the woman, took her to the waiting room and administered soothing words, telling her that the child would be perfectly all right. In the ordinary way she would have left it to one of her staff nurses and Staff

Nurse Burton, seated in the nursing station, smiled at another passing staff nurse meaningly. Carmichael was aware of this and felt herself flushing. Was she perhaps overdoing it, she wondered.

Then there was the inevitable overdose dealt with by staff nurse and Casualty officer. The stomach was washed out, and the anxious, tearful relatives were interviewed and the patient was removed to the medical ward following the usual argument on the telephone with the ward sister who insisted that there were no beds available.

There were a number of cut fingers and this morning the usual twisted ankle, wrist, various fractures and, a little more dramatically, a woman who had run over her foot with a lawn-mower.

During the morning the examination rooms were rarely vacant. The Casualty officers were in and out and the ward clerk was kept busy. Nurses hurried about briskly, perhaps infected by their senior sister's eagle eye and stimulated by the presence of the new consultant.

Lunchtime came and it was only then that the two doctors left the department. Nigel Denton turned pleasantly to Carmichael as he passed her, saying; 'I'll be back, Sister, and we'll have a long pow-wow, have a word about – where was it? – St Jude's, wasn't it?'

Carmichael had nodded, pleased that two of her staff nurses had heard. The moment he went through the door they turned to her and one of them said; 'Oh, know him, do you, Sister? A good-looker, isn't he? Is he nice to work for?

Carmichael turned to her with an unaccustomed smile.

'Oh yes, very nice, a charming man. I'm sure he'll be a great asset to the hospital and to this Casualty department.

It was not her usual stiff reply and it made one of the other staff nurses giggle as she turned away.

Carmichael wondered, she wondered a lot of things about Nigel Denton. She wondered if he had got over all his problems. It was years ago, of course, but even so experiences such as those he had had left a mark on a man. She would not mention anything at all, the past was a secret between her and Nigel Denton and secrets always made Carmichael feel more powerful, less vulnerable. She straightened her back and at that moment Sister Taylor walked past.

'Busy morning, Agnes,' she said brightly. She was a pretty girl, Carmichael thought, tall and rather willowy. Her hair, in Carmichael's view, was always a trifle too long, nevertheless it was always tidy. Her trim waist encircled by its black belt and silver buckle enhanced her rather slender appearance which had made Carmichael at first wonder whether or not she was strong enough for the demanding job. She soon found out that she was unflagging and always cheerful. Carmichael had at first disliked the girl's make-up, she thought it a trace heavy. She had spoken to her about it and Taylor had shown her even temperament by reducing the eye-shadow and lipstick slightly, but not doing away with them completely. She smelled too of a pleasant perfume. It was hardly discernible, but when she went by Carmichael was always aware of it and she was sure that the doctors were too.

Now when they were less busy was the time, Carmichael felt, to ask about her relationship with the new orthopaedic consultant.

'Have you known Mr Denton long, Madeleine?' she asked, using the Christian name self-consciously, for she did not often do so.

'Oh yes, some time now,' Madeleine Taylor replied, keeping her eyes cast down and her face expressionless.

'Where did you meet him?' Carmichael felt she was prying but could not stop herself.

Taylor looked up and their eyes met. She hesitated before replying, but then she spoke in her usual lively manner with a slight smile – and just a touch of mischief, Carmichael thought.

'Well, Agnes, you could say that we bumped into each other, literally. We were skiing in Austria.' She left it there but Carmichael could not.

'Oh, I see,' she said and continued to look at Madeleine Taylor who blushed slightly.

'Oh no, I don't think you do, Sister Carmichael, not really.' She turned on her heel and walked away.

'An affair,' thought Carmichael. 'An affair, positively, that's what it is.' Then she wondered if it was still going on, and just what they meant to each other. She didn't like it. Carmichael did not approve of affairs between members of staff. It affected their work and caused speculation among the rest of the staff. An affair between a consultant and a nurse was anything but satisfactory.

She dismissed some of her staff to lunch and watched Staff Nurse Burton leave the department with Nurse Pearson. She saw them link arms at the door and wondered at their friendliness. In her junior days one hadn't been friendly like that, not a staff nurse with an auxiliary nurse. Still, it was all different now.

She went back to her office and picked up her cloak. It was a warm day, and the spring sunshine made the cloak unnecessary, but, as usual, Carmichael would not be seen anywhere without it. She knew people remarked on it but it made no difference. She flung it round her shoulders and said to Madeleine Taylor: 'If Mr Denton comes back tell him I won't be long, I'll come back from lunch early. He said on his way out that he wanted to talk to me.'

'Oh Lord, Agnes, I wouldn't start spoiling him. He'll have to fit in with our ways a bit you know. I mean, we've got to have our meal times. I wouldn't come back early, really I wouldn't.' Madeleine Taylor looked at her with a slight twist of mischief again as if she knew what she was saying was quite useless and that Carmichael would probably be back a quarter-of-an-hour early to see if Nigel Denton was there – just in case.

'I expect he's married.' The remark was jerked out of Carmichael almost to her surprise.

'No,' Sister Taylor answered gently, as if seeing into Carmichael's mind. 'He's a widower, actually.'

'Nurse has got the report book at the station. If you go and ask her she will tell you what has been in and what is still in X-ray and if we're expecting anything.'

'OK,' said Sister Taylor, 'will do.' She walked towards the middle of the department where the nurse sat idly filing her nails – a fact which Carmichael did not miss.

She turned round again and called after Sister Taylor: ' . . . and tell her we don't attend to our toilet in the Casualty department, will you please, Sister.'

33

Sister Taylor nodded, grimaced and made her way up to the nurse to get the report and presumably to reprimand her. Carmichael swept out.

The dining room in this huge complex housed the consultants, junior doctors, sisters, nurses, administrators, domestics and maintenance staff. It was very large and divided by glass partitions behind which people segregated themselves. Carmichael had never found out if it was a rule, for there were no labels saying 'doctors' or 'nurses' or 'managerial staff' or anything else, it just seemed to happen that way naturally: doctors did not sit with sisters and sisters did not sit with nurses.

She made her way to the place where the sisters congregated, took a vacant chair, looked at the menu, and told a green-clad worker that she would have the steak and kidney pie. It was brought to her almost immediately and put down in front of her with a slight bang so that some of the gravy splashed over the tablecloth. She looked up to give the woman a quick word of reproof and she noticed that it was one of the demonstrators who had jeered a little the previous day when she had gone past them through the door into the hospital. This was probably just a show of malice, so Carmichael said nothing.

She spoke infrequently to the other sisters about anything personal, she didn't talk much at all but whenever she did it was about the hospital, about work.

Suddenly a sister at the other end of the table leaned forward and said loudly: 'Peeping Tom there last night? A flasher too we heard. You saw him, didn't you, Carmichael? A ghastly sight?'

'It was pretty disgusting,' said Carmichael, 'but no doubt the police will catch up with him shortly.'

'Did he actually flash? You know, show you all he'd got?' asked a younger sister sitting next to Carmichael, her eyes twinkling, her rather untidy black curly hair almost obliterating her cap. 'What was he like? I mean, you know.'

'He was medium height, dark-haired, nothing particularly remarkable about him. He was wearing a long, black coat.' Carmichael picked primly at her meal. 'That was all I saw and I told the police accordingly.'

'Oh, no distinguishing feature, eh? I mean he didn't have . . .

say an appendix scar, or a mole somewhere or other?' The sister was obviously laughing at Carmichael and some of the others joined in.

Carmichael felt anger rising in her for no real reason. They obviously wanted her to make some remark about his genitals. She turned to the sister sitting beside her and looked her levelly in the eye.

'He was made as any other man is, I presume,' she said.

'You presume? Don't you know then? I should have thought you would have nursed one or two males, dear.'

The sister opposite, who was fat, and who looked rather like Carmichael's friend Jones, laughed heartily.

Carmichael did not answer, but the remark and the likeness of the sister to Jones brought back the memory of her friend's letter. To think she was now a nursing officer and here she was, still sitting at the sisters' table. Well, she wasn't going to let that get her down. She did not speak again and when she had finished her steak and kidney pie and refused the sweet, she got up and left the dining room. As she did so she heard one of the sisters say to the younger one who had been sitting beside her: 'You offended old Carmichael, you are a twit. She's . . . well I don't think she's had . . .you know what I mean.'

'You mean she's a calcified virgin, don't you? Well, that's no fault of mine.'

'No, perhaps not, but you could lay off her a bit. It wasn't too nice what you said and she was embarrassed.'

Carmichael heard all this before she left the dining room and again a furious hatred arose in her towards women who could handle men, handle the situation that always seemed to arise between men and women, talk to them, not worry about sex or . . . Well, they were right, she was a virgin. If only Harry . . . she wouldn't have been a virgin then, wouldn't have wanted to be. Some of them would have anybody, she thought, they'd have sex with just anyone. She closed down the thoughts. No more of that, she said to herself.

She made her way towards her own department again. She would not go up and have coffee in the rest room, but go back in case she missed Nigel Denton. She didn't want him to get a first impression of the department from Madeleine Taylor. She suddenly felt intensely depressed. Oh yes, she would see him now, talk to him now perhaps, but it was Madeleine Taylor he really wanted to see and talk to. He would look on her, as they'd said in the dining room, as an 'old girl'. That's what they called her, even in Casualty, and she knew it.

She was half-way along the corridor when she met the nursing officer, Miss Thompson, accompanied by an attractive-looking man. It was Miss Thompson who had got the job in this hospital for which Carmichael had applied.

She was a pleasant girl, and although Carmichael resented her youth she did not resent her in any other way for she was neither pretty nor attractive. A woman who had no claim to good looks rather endeared herself to Carmichael. She stopped as Carmichael was going by and said: 'Oh, Sister, may I introduce Mr Hanson, Mr Derek Hanson. He's our new fire officer. He'll be coming round to see you, in fact he'll be seeing everybody, he's got rather a large job with a lot of ground to cover.' She looked at him and smiled, but his eyes were on Carmichael's face as she gazed at him.

He was a well-built man of – Carmichael guessed – about forty-five or perhaps a little more. His hair, which had been black, was now greying rather attractively at the temples. His face was handsome, he had an alert look and was slightly tanned as if he had spent time in the tropics. His eyes were brown and were, Carmichael thought, perhaps his worst feature, for they were hard, and looked at her as if he was boring through her head to see what was inside. His mouth, slightly covered by a moustache, smiled widely revealing white even teeth. Carmichael was momentarily transfixed by his mouth: his lips were red and beautifully shaped, moist, rather feminine, yet Carmichael was acutely aware of his masculinity.

'Sister Carmichael. And where . . .?'

'Sister Carmichael is senior sister in Casualty,' said Miss Thompson.

'Ah yes, we have to watch all the fire hazards there, don't we, Sister Carmichael? Miss Thompson has been kind enough to show me your department but I shall want to come back and examine it more carefully.'

Carmichael nodded but did not answer. She felt acutely

uncomfortable in this man's presence and could not quite understand her own feelings. His next question rather startled her.

'Are you married, Sister? Do you live away from the hospital?'

Carmichael paused for a moment before she replied and this gave him time to justify his question.

'Forgive me, I'm not being idly curious. It's just that I like to know those who live on the premises, it's all part of my job.'

'Sister Carmichael lives in the nurses' home. She used to have a country cottage before she came here when she was working in her last hospital. I believe it was very lovely from what she tells me. She has described it to me but you've sold it now haven't you, Sister?'

'Yes I have.' Carmichael felt that her privacy was being invaded and yet he was right, of course. He would want to know who lived in. Still, he could surely have found that out from a list. Perhaps he was just making conversation, after all, he had a new job and a lot of people to meet. Yes, that was probably it. She withdrew her eyes from his with difficulty and looked at her nursing officer.

'I must get back. We've got our new orthopaedic consultant today. He wants to have a chat with me and I expect there will be plenty to talk about.'

'Oh yes, I've got to see him too. We made a date to have a cup of tea together.' Miss Thompson's remark included the fire officer and Carmichael wondered why she bothered. After all it was no concern of his.

'I see,' said Hanson. 'Well, I mustn't keep you,' and they walked on.

Carmichael felt a vague annoyance at the meeting, and annoyance too that Nigel Denton had made arrangements to have tea with her nursing officer. She suddenly remembered in much greater detail the night at St Jude's when they'd had the bus crash and all available staff had gone to Casualty to help, when even Marion Hughes and the consultants had done their bit. It had been a wonderfully dramatic night and Carmichael had been so enjoying it until Marion Hughes had discovered that she was there and had reprimanded her for leaving her

37

ward to come and help. But then Nigel Denton had stuck up for her and praised the work she had done in Casualty. Well, Marion Hughes had suffered for that reprimand and suffered badly, suffered as much as anybody could be made to.

Carmichael continued on her way to Casualty. When she got there there was no sign of Nigel Denton. It was much too early, he was probably still having lunch with the rest of the consultants. But she had not seen him in the dining room. Madeleine Taylor looked up as she came in.

'Gracious, you've only had a few minutes for lunch, you are keen. I've let Nurse Wilson go early, hope you don't mind but there was a phone call, some complication about her mother being taken to hospital, not this, some other hospital. She's broken her hip. I expect she'll land up here eventually.'

'You should have sent a message to me in the dining room,' said Carmichael tartly.

'Well, by the look of it you probably would have already left. By the way the nursing officer brought a chap along here, quite a handsome brute, he's to be the new fire officer. I've heard all the hospitals are having one. He's not very young but he's dishy. What the dickens he'll do I don't know. Go round inspecting our fire-extinguishers I expect. Do you remember that day . . .?' She started to laugh uncontrollably.

Carmichael did remember the day to which she was referring but as usual couldn't see anything humorous about it. One of the nursing officers had taken a fire-extinquisher to the front door to demonstrate it to some of the nurses and something had backfired and had hit her and knocked her unconscious much to the amusement of the staff once they had seen that she was not seriously hurt. Yes, Carmichael did remember but she made no remark about it and turned and walked to her own office to wait for Nigel Denton, aware that Madeleine Taylor had shrugged her shoulders in mock despair because Carmichael had walked away without a smile.

7

Although Nigel Denton and Madeleine Taylor were more than acquainted, this couldn't detract from the fact that Carmichael had known him before in another hospital; it gave her a feeling of superiority over the other sisters. It pleased her to know that the link existed, that she could say whenever she wished; 'Yes, I knew Mr Denton, we worked in the same hospital.' She even toyed with the idea of saying: 'I knew Nigel', but habit forbade her to do this. She needn't go into details, she needn't say that then she had been only a crushed, miserable staff nurse. It gave her a warm, comfortable feeling to know that he was at least an acquaintance of hers, though in her heart she knew she could hardly call him even that. It would be seen soon enough that Nigel Denton and Sister Taylor were . . . well, that was something that for the moment she chose to put on one side.

Denton did not arrive in the department until three o'clock. This annoyed Carmichael because her junior sister had had time to go to lunch and return to the department. However, she was taken up with a patient when Nigel Denton walked in. They were not as busy as usual and this too slightly annoyed Carmichael. She would have liked Casualty to have been really busy when he arrived, really buzzing as it had been this morning. Only six of the examination rooms were occupied and the nurses were walking about in a leisurely fashion; one carrying a kidney dish with an empty syringe in it almost bumped into the consultant as he entered Casualty. Again this irritated Carmichael for he took the nurse's arm to steady her after the impact, in what Carmichael judged to be a very familiar way.

'Watch out now or you'll have another casualty on your

hands,' he said, and the nurse smiled rather shyly at him and he smiled warmly back. He likes women, thought Carmichael waspishly.

'Anything interesting in, Sister?' He greeted Carmichael without mentioning her name and she immediately assumed he'd forgotten it.

'Not really, just the usual things. One small boy has been kicked over the nose by a horse – just a graze on the skin, the nose is not broken. He was lucky to escape its hoof. He has been X-rayed, but I thought . . .'

'Well, he's one for a good dose of anti-tetanus eh, Sister?' said Nigel Denton lightly.

'I don't know what you mean by a good dose, he's just had the usual dose we give on such occasions.' Carmichael replied so coldly, so frostily that Nigel Denton looked momentarily startled, then pretended to back away from her as if in mock fear and said, 'Sorry, Sister,' and made his way towards the doctor's office. He walked in ahead of her, motioning to her to sit down in the chair opposite him.

'I've had a word with the Casualty officer, Dr Singh,' he said as he sat down. 'He seems very satisfied about the way the department is run. He also luckily gets on well with Dr Jones. It's nice when the Casualty officers agree even if agreeing to differ, isn't it, Sister Carmichael?' He grimaced slightly and his eyes twinkled, the laughter lines round them deepened. Carmichael found herself simpering but was not altogether reassured by his charm.

'This is a very efficiently built and planned department, I like the lay-out,' he went on, and as she appeared to be preoccupied he said her name again. Carmichael at last was reassured that he did remember, and she softened a little. If he'd remembered her name after all, well, that was something, even if he'd remembered only from when the orthopaedic surgeon introduced her today, but she hoped that he now recollected her from St Jude's.

'Yes, it is, I mean it was carefully thought-out. After all, it should be, the hospital is new.'

'Yes, that is so, Sister, but these days they seem to be almost obsolete before they've finished building them, don't they?'

Carmichael picked up a pen from the desk and doodled idly on the clean blotting pad, something she would not normally do, but she felt nervous, uncomfortable as she always did when talking to a man.

'If there's anything you need, anything you think should be altered, just tell me. It's the time to get it done when a new consultant comes along, isn't it?' He looked up quickly as he spoke and again his eyes with those crinkly lines round them met hers and his smile was pleasant, but as he smiled Carmichael caught a whiff of alcohol on his breath and remembered St Jude's again. Well, maybe this was just from a glass of sherry that he'd had before lunch, no doubt he'd be offered one, particularly as he'd just arrived. Even so . . .

'Indeed I will. There are one or two things, quite small but I expect you'll be able to help me with them.'

'Yes, we'll talk about that when I have more time, I'm just getting to know the place at the moment. Are you adequately staffed, do you feel?' He went on: 'Sister Taylor is on duty when you're off, I presume. Is that right, Sister Carmichael?'

Carmichael half agreed, her head inclined in acquiescence but her face looking slightly doubtful.

'Yes, that is mostly. When she has her days off and I have mine; of course, we have to have our usual daily off duty and we don't work a full day, so there may be times when the staff nurses cover but they're perfectly able to, I see to that – I train them for that,' said Carmichael.

'Yes, I realize that, and we've got the nursing officer should we need her in an emergency – Miss Thompson isn't it?'

'Yes, but she's only on duty from nine till five you know. Whoever is in trauma section has to act up when she's off duty or Sister Taylor or I are, you understand that?'

'I have been working in this situation for some time, Sister. I certainly do realize how the system works.'

To Carmichael this sounded like a rebuff and she momentarily recoiled, wishing she had put the remark in another way. Whether it was because of that or for some other reason, he made no reference at all to St Jude's, or to the fact that they had met and that they had worked together, well, at least once, at another hospital. Either it had gone out of his head or

Carmichael had not pleased him, she couldn't be sure.

He got up and she rose too and they went out into the department, she to get on with her work and he to look round. She didn't quite know whether he wanted her to remain with him or not, so she left him, filled with a vague feeling of dissatisfaction. She watched him walk down the lines of examination rooms, parting the curtains to peep inside, and Carmichael was not made to feel any better by the fact that Madeleine Taylor came out of one examination room as he did this and greeted him with a smile. She had on the usual thin plastic apron and gloves that the nurses used when they were doing dressings or dealing with a casualty.

'Mr Denton,' she said archly and Nigel Denton laughed. She was flushed and looked to Carmichael, as no doubt she did to Nigel Denton, very attractive.

'Happy at your work, Sister?' Madeleine Taylor smiled a wide smile.

'Yes, fairly so, Mr Denton,' she said. 'Fairly. I like it busier than this, but I don't wish the population any harm and, of course, I like the whole set-up better since the appointment of the new consultant.'

It was obviously said in fun but Carmichael felt, as usual, stabbed by jealousy. She noticed as she did so often the easy traffic of light conversation, badinage, between men and women, something she seemed never to manage herself. Why was it she felt this stiffness, a self-consciousness every time she had to talk to a man, even a young house officer or porter? She always felt it and she hated it. When she watched the easy interchange between her nurses and any man she was always filled with envy at their ability to act as if there was no sex barrier. The nurses managed to charm, to flirt, or sometimes to treat men in a perfectly ordinary brotherly or sisterly way. Why couldn't she? It was something that had haunted her all her adult life. She had hoped that as she grew older this would disappear and she would forget it, but it wasn't so.

She went into her office and sat down at her desk and tapped idly with the tip of her pen. The thought of the fire officer again came in to her mind: Derek Hanson – she said his name quietly under her breath. Why was she thinking of him? His duties?

Would she see anything of him in Casualty? She supposed so, he would have work to do all over the hospital, fire-escapes to inspect, emergency exits, fire-extinguishers, she supposed he'd conduct fire-drill too. Yes, she was bound to see him, but why was she thinking of him? Would she be happier with him as against other men? If she met him again would she be able to . . .? After all, he looked older than her and had a certain military swagger. She felt again self-conscious at the very thought of him. She dismissed him almost violently from her mind.

That afternoon Carmichael did something she very rarely did. In her office in the Casualty department she wrote a personal letter. If she had caught any of her nurses doing this she would have come down on them heavily. The letter was to Sister Jones congratulating her on her promotion to nursing officer and also suggesting that she should come to Carmichael's hospital for a weekend now that she, Jones, would have every weekend free.

She would show Jones round the hospital; she was sure Jones would be interested and impressed. She went on in this way and ended the letter as usual: 'Yours sincerely, Agnes Carmichael.'

It would be Jones's first visit to this great hospital and Carmichael felt she needed to show off the Casualty department that she ran. It was so much bigger, she was sure, than anything Jones had ever seen. She sealed the letter with some satisfaction, unlocked the drawer in which she kept her handbag, took out a stamp from her purse and stuck it on the letter, then put it in her bag ready for posting after she had finished her duty. She felt better after writing the letter, it was ridiculous to feel jealous of Jones. After all, nursing officer was nothing – moving a few nurses about when someone went off sick or someone didn't turn up for duty – compared with running this department with its sixteen examination rooms, theatres and so on. It was like a little world and Jones couldn't possibly have any knowledge of what it entailed. Carmichael felt she couldn't wait to have her friend here and show her round.

It would be pleasant, too, to have Jones stay in the nurses' home in the guest room, a change from having her at her cottage as she had done on several occasions before. Carmichael sat there day-dreaming. Again this was not a thing she did often, particularly when she was on duty, but she was thinking of the cottage she had left and then of the cottage she would get some time in the future, after retirement perhaps, with a slightly larger kitchen and even a larger garden too. She would look for a cottage with a larger second bedroom – in her last cottage the spare room had been so very small. And when she retired she wouldn't want to live in such a secluded lane, after all one got older and one had to think of that – somewhere, perhaps, nearer the town because, after all, it would be the last cottage she would buy, it would be the place where she would spend the rest of her days. As she thought this, the lonely life in front of her seemed almost as if it could be touched, the thought of living alone, watching the television night after night, getting up in the morning . . .well it was not yet, not for many years. Carmichael tried to brush this thought away. Too many of her thoughts were unpleasant nowadays, she decided, and tried to find a pleasant one. Again, strangely enough, her thoughts returned to Derek Hanson.

The rest of the afternoon was busier. A man came in with a piece of glass in his cornea, which necessitated calling Miss Haskins who worked in the eye department and then the eye consultant, Mr Jevons, a taciturn and, it was rumoured, a difficult man to work for. But, of course, everything went off well when he was attended by Carmichael. Her propitiatory manner, the way she constantly called him 'sir', seemed to make him more pleasant. He even gave her a wintry smile as he left the department having recommended that the patient be admitted to the eye ward.

After he had left one of her staff nurses said teasingly, 'You get on well with old Jevons, Sister Carmichael, which is more than anyone else does, or so I hear.'

This earned the nurse a rebuke for using the word 'old', but for all that Carmichael was pleased by the remark.

During the afternoon hardly any of the examination rooms were free. A child with a bee-sting on the tongue had to be admitted, bawling fearfully. Carmichael watched her nurses without once getting the feeling that she was inferior to her friend Jones. No, she was superior, this was a real post. Nursing officer in St Matthew's was just nothing. Well, she was in a position to know.

She was more than usually watchful that afternoon and even the Casualty officers looked at her with some apprehension as they went about their tasks, taking blood, filling in X-ray forms, talking to patients' relatives. Carmichael became more and more conscious that she was very much in charge here, very much the ruler – even Madeleine Taylor had to watch out. The junior sister had gone off duty but would be back again in the evening. Split duties were rare in this hospital, but they sometimes had to take place if Carmichael decreed it – another thing in which she differed from the other sisters. It had been suggested several times at sisters' meetings that split duty should be done away with, and it had almost vanished from all the other wards and departments. Indeed, her own nursing officer had tried rather feebly to argue her out of the habit, and eventually split duties might be abolished altogether by a higher authority. Well, thought Carmichael, so be it, but meanwhile she clung to her own ways. They were trying to push her into line, but Carmichael knew her rights and if she wanted Sister Taylor to be on duty when she herself was off, and this meant doing a split duty now and again, that was how she would have it. If she was finally overruled by the chief nursing officer then she, Carmichael, would have to put up with it. Meanwhile it was a fight, a little battle, and Carmichael always found battles exhilarating.

8

Outside the spring evening was already turning to darkness but the lights from the hospital windows and the lamps dotted here and there in the grounds made everything an eerie blue. As Carmichael made her way from the hospital towards the nurses' home, she thought the lights there coming from the downstairs windows would keep the Peeping Tom away, away from that side of the home anyway. The other side, the garden side, was not so well lit. There were some lights on the drive going down to the home, but none on the far side. Carmichael thought of suggesting at the next sisters' meeting that more lighting should be put round at the back of the home, but she wondered whether her experience and that of the nurses would justify the expense.

In spite of the semi-darkness, Carmichael felt no fear, but she walked quickly and as an insurance clutched her handbag rather tightly under her arm. After all, she thought, if that man was interested in stealing he might . . . but she arrived at the nurses' home door without mishap and went to her room.

A glance in the mirror made her decide to wash her hair, then she remembered that she had again forgotten to see if there was any post as she came in; if she washed her hair this evening it might to useful to have a hairbrush. She made her way out of her room again, prudently locking her door behind her as she nearly always did, went to the front hall and looked in the post-rack to see if there was anything for her. There was a small packet bearing the name of the firm from which she had ordered the brush. She took it with satisfaction. There was no other post for her, but then she did not expect it. Carmichael had few people to keep up a correspondence with, even in her last hospital she hadn't really made many friends, no one who would write to her or come and see her. She felt that she preferred it that way, things had happened in her last hospital that she wished to forget. Anyway, she preferred not to meet people from her past, apart from Jones, fat Jones, and she somehow did not seem to matter.

Friends, too, expected things to happen to one over a period of time. Most of the women she knew talked about their husbands or their boyfriends, or men they wished were their boyfriends, or the men they were living with. She had nothing to contribute to that kind of conversation. If it wasn't that, they talked of their parents, their brothers or their sisters, or about a family wedding they'd been to. No, it was better, Carmichael thought, when you were utterly alone to remain that way. If you joined in and tried to make friends with people who had families it was hopeless, there was nothing to compare notes about.

She turned on her heel, splitting open the package as she did so. Suddenly the door of the home burst open and two nurses tumbled in, half screaming, half laughing and yet frightened.

'Oh, Sister Carmichael, we've seen him tonight, the one you saw. You saw him, didn't you, he's outside, we've just seen him. He's just outside the door. He was hiding round the corner. He's just like you said, a flasher, we saw everything,' cried one of the nurses. Now that they were safely inside their faces were resuming their normal colour. They both began to giggle but nervously and hysterically.

'What shall we do, Sister Carmichael? I mean we just ran in. I don't know what he did or where he went to. I don't think he'll come in, will he?' They suddenly both turned round and looked at the glass door. 'Perhaps he went round to peer in the windows at the back like he did when he saw you. We heard about him on C4, someone told us. He's just like you said. We could see him in the light from the home door plainly. I don't know what he thinks he's up to, someone will catch him.'

Carmichael nodded. 'I'll telephone the hospital, you go to your rooms,' she said authoritatively. She had no jurisdiction over nurses in the home, seniority meant nothing here, but nevertheless she automatically took charge and the nurses

47

turned obediently toward the staircase still clutching each other. They were young, still half frightened and silly, Carmichael thought loftily. Remembering what the man had looked like when she had seen him she was not really surprised at their pallor and their hysterical screaming and giggling as they'd come through the door. She rang the hospital and got the night superintendent who had just come on duty. He sighed heavily when Carmichael reported that the Peeping Tom was about again.

'Very well, Sister, I suppose I shall have to call Mr Stewart again. Then we'll get the police here. It's really too much isn't it? He'll be gone by the time they get here and Mr Stewart won't be best pleased having his evening interrupted. I'm bound to get it in the neck. Can you have a look outside yourself?'

'I certainly cannot and will not,' said Carmichael. 'It's not my job and I've had the unpleasant sight once, I don't want it again, thank you. Of course he will be gone but the police must come. We can't be sure, he may be round at the back of the home now. It's their duty to come, even the nurses who saw him thought he might still be here.' She put the phone down abruptly and was about to enter her own room when she stopped and listened for a few moments. She could hear the nurses still talking, going from room to room telling other nurses. She thought she might warn them that they would have to be interviewed by the police as she had been, but decided against it. As she stood there another nurse came through the door and Carmichael turned quickly. This was an older women whom Carmichael did not know. She looked quite composed and glanced at Carmichael inquiringly.

'Did you see anything outside, a man? There's that Peeping Tom about, well I think they call him a flasher.' Carmichael said.

'I didn't see anyone, Sister, not that I was looking. I didn't see a soul out there. Why, what's happened?'

'Oh, two nurses were frightened by him just now. I've seen him once, he's disgusting. He must be caught. I've rung the hospital. The police will be here again, I expect. I'm not sure which rooms the nurses went to. I suppose I'd better find out . . . No, I won't, let the police do it.' Carmichael stalked along to her own room and when the police car eventually made its way up the drive she did not emerge until there was a knock on the door. It was the night superintendent.

'Ah, Sister Carmichael, what a nuisance this is. I've found those two nurses, they're upstairs in their room chatting away to everybody of course and they say they won't sleep all night. There's a whole bevy round them, drinking tea and gossiping.'

'They were a bit hysterical when they came in. They said they'd seen him outside the front door. He did the usual thing, I suppose, then ran away.'

'Well, that at least confirms your story, doesn't it?' said the night superintendent. He was a man nearing his retirement, a matter-of-fact, practical sort without any kind of charm or breeding, Carmichael thought.

'I hardly think my story needed confirming, did it?' she asked. 'Did they think it was something that all happened in my imagination?'

The night super looked at her quickly. Carmichael was amused, guessing that he thought he was speaking to a difficult woman. Well, he was right.

'No, no, of course not. But it's nice to have it corroborated, isn't it? I mean, now that three people have seen him that really will get the police on the go. They're going to leave someone here for a few hours tonight patrolling the grounds with a dog.'

'I should think so and I've never, never needed any story of mine corroborated before. I saw the man and that's that. It doesn't matter how many nurses see him now it's a fact and they should have known that when I said I saw him, I saw him. I immediately reported it.'

'Oh, they did, of course they believed you, but you know how the police are. They think, well, sometimes, that a woman could be imagining it. They think women are not always reliable.'

'Do they? And men too?' asked Carmichael, even more sharply.

'I expect so,' said the night super vaguely, not realizing that he was on very tender ground with Carmichael, very tender ground indeed, but he was sensitive enough to realize that he had upset her and he withdrew more hastily than he had intended.

'Well, I'll leave you to get a good night's sleep. They said the same as before, that everyone should keep their windows shut. I should think you could open the top a bit but if this goes on all the downstairs windows will have to be locked.'

'A very good idea. Locks were fitted when the home was built,' said Carmichael coldly and, almost without giving him time to leave, pushed the door to. He heard the latch click.

Corroboration indeed! Carmichael was furious. She finished opening the package and took out the brush. It looked utterly useless, but still, her hair couldn't look worse, she thought, bending down and looking again in the mirror of her dressing table. She felt for a moment the familiar almost tangible loneliness that came over her when people said something to make her doubt her integrity. She was suddenly glad that the two nurses had seen the man, glad that now they knew she wasn't 'seeing things' or exaggerating. She suddenly thought of Harry and of being in love, of the wonderful feeling of confidence she had when she was beside him, that most wonderful, sublime and beautiful feeling, the best she had ever had. Would she ever again feel for a man as she had for Harry Maitland? In anguish she suddenly sat down at the dressing table and addressed her own image.

'Oh, if it had only been me whom he had liked, if he'd fallen in love with me and not Margaret. But I wasn't right for him, was I? I wasn't suitable, I didn't know enough about etiquette and dinner tables and restaurants . . . I wasn't upper class.'

As she sat gazing at herself she remembered the gateau that had fallen on the floor in the restaurant, she had knocked it out of the waitress's hand, and how Emily had . . . Emily had done everything so right. She shivered suddenly and got to her feet. She must wash her hair, half dry it and then use her new hairbrush. Maybe it would do something. She gave another glance in the mirror, her face had not changed much over the years, the nose was still too long, pointed, and for ever reddened at the tip. No matter what cosmetics she used it was always red at the tip, there seemed nothing she could do about it. She'd tried mascara on her sandy lashes but it made her look ridiculous, in fact any make-up she put on stood out on her white skin. Perhaps she wasn't skilful enough about the foundation, perhaps she ought to get in touch with an expert. There was a hairdresser and beautician in the town where there were occasionally demonstrators who made you up, using cosmetics from well-known firms. Yes, she would try that. Why not? She'd see what they did, after all she could wash her face before she came home if it didn't look nice.

Suddenly Carmichael was seized with the idea to start again, to try and make herself over, look more attractive, really try. She looked down at her hands. They were nice, she always manicured her nails carefully, wore colourless varnish and always used plenty of hand lotion. She would not permit even pale pink nail varnish on her nurses so she couldn't use it herself. On the wards, of course, they were allowed to . . . Yes, she would make a real effort, she would do her hair with this brush tonight, following the instructions on the little piece of paper enclosed with it. Then tomorrow was her half day and she would go into the town and make an appointment to consult one of the beauticians who would know more about make-up than she did.

Then she asked herself why, why was she doing all this. For no reason at all, she thought and shrugged her shoulders. But how did she know who would look at her? Someone might, though more probably nobody would think of asking her out to a meal. Most of the doctors were so much younger than she was and the consultants, well, they were married.

Carmichael pulled herself up short. What was she thinking of? Well, it didn't matter, but she decided to follow the dictates of her own mind, knowing very well that into whatever strange places they led she would usually follow. Suddenly she knew why she was thinking all this, it was the fire officer, Derek Hanson. She remembered again his bold brown eyes staring at her, his appraisal. Well, after all, he wasn't much, only a fire officer, but there'd been something about him. He was nothing like Harry – nobody would ever be like Harry, that was in the past – but if she looked nice enough and played her cards right, after all he wasn't everybody's cup of tea, he wasn't young, fifty at least . . . She gave herself a familiar little shake. Why not?

After all I can try, some men don't think only about looks and sex, they think of intelligence and the ability to do a job.

Carmichael went through into the little bathroom, talking aloud to herself. 'He's older than me.' She felt rather silly talking aloud, but she didn't feel silly enough to stop herself smiling as she ran the water to wash her hair.

When she came out of the bathroom, her head wrapped in a towel, she sat again at her dressing table, took the towel from her head and surveyed herself. Her hair now looked darker. Did it suit her that way? Should she have it tinted a little? She decided against it, her hair was flat on her head and so thin, but she knew that as it dried it would get thicker-looking, if only for a day. Perhaps she should wash it every night? She did not look her best at the moment. Despair struck again, but then she thought that such a lot could be done with make-up. She never tried enough. Oh, she had a little when Harry . . . but then he'd been blind. She remembered her perfume and wondered if she should start using that again or a new one. She didn't approve of that kind of thing, but just a touch, just so that when she went by she left a slight fragrance behind her like Sister Taylor. Why not? She was too stiff, too nursey. She must make herself . . . teach herself to look at men with that long look. Even the youngest nurses could do it.

Even as she thought this she realized she had been thinking the same thing for twenty years; for twenty years she had been trying to flirt and had never succeeded. But this time she was going to try harder. She would unbend, particularly to the new fire officer, she would concentrate on him. He would be, well, he would be someone, a man to practise on.

Carmichael gazed critically at the face in front of her. How did quite ugly women achieve a sort of beauty? Eyeshadow, tinted face powder, a tiny touch of rouge on the chin, night cream faithfully used, moisturizing cream, cuticle and hand creams, anti-wrinkle cream. Really it all boiled down to how much you were willing to spend.

She pulled herself up smartly, realizing it was all getting out of hand. Was she doing all this, thinking of spending a lot of money on herself, just because of Derek Hanson? Yes, she was.

52

'Come along now, Agnes, don't be silly,' she said aloud. 'But then, after all, you've nothing to lose, you don't care for him and that is where you score, you don't care for him as you did for Harry, so it won't hurt – not this time, even if he takes no notice of you, it won't hurt.'

She remembered about the letter to Jones still in her handbag, she would post it tomorrow. By the time Jones came she might have changed quite a bit for the better, she might even have a man, someone she dated. Jones would be surprised.

9

True to her resolution, Carmichael arranged an appointment at Antoinette's salon. She had not been there before and, as she entered the door, the warmth and the smell of expensive perfume slightly overlaid by the more acrid smell of perm lotion, momentarily halted her. An exquisite young woman behind the desk looked at her inquiringly, her perfectly plucked eyebrows slightly raised.

'Do you have an appointment, madam?' she asked through equally perfectly rouged lips

'I have an appointment, shampoo and set, facial and eyebrow plucking – Miss Carmichael.'

'With anyone in particular?'

'No. I . . .'

'I see, madam.' The young woman nodded understandingly and Carmichael felt the girl had already summed her up as a newcomer, an amateur in the beauty salon business. She pointed with a silver lacquered nail: 'Will you hang your coat in there and put on a . . . ' She turned away as another client approached.

Carmichael did as she was instructed but stood uncertainly, not sure how to put the gown on. Then, seeing the woman who had followed her up to the reception desk shed her coat, put on the lavender robe and pick up a magazine, she did the same. She followed the woman to a row of chairs and sat down. The woman did not look at her. Already Carmichael felt humiliated and resentful. It crossed her mind that Margaret Tarrant or Emily Maitland would have known what to do and been quite at home in these circumstances. She squared her shoulders. Well, her money was as good as anyone else's. She would find out, she would not be put off by the expensive look of the place, the perfume and the heavily made-up young woman at the reception desk.

Carmichael had reserved enough time to have her hair done, have a facial, have her face made up and her eyebrows plucked. It was all going to be very expensive. She'd tried before with her hair, she'd been to various hairdressers, had permanent waves, had it cut by people who were supposed to be great specialists in the art, who had trained in Paris, so they had said. They had always assured her that they could make her hair much more easy to cope with. 'Just a little movement,' they said before they permed it, 'just a little movement will make all the difference', but it always came out frizzy. In her own estimation, after the perm had grown out her hair always remained the same and the 'little movement' they talked about was never a success.

She was in the salon for two-and-a-half hours and, having paid an enormous bill, came out with a distinctive Antoinette plastic bag containing innumerable pots of night and day cream, foundation cream, bottles of lotions, shampoos and conditioners. She was determined to use them all exactly as the girl had instructed, every night and every morning, and when she made a decision, Carmichael thought to herself proudly, she usually carried it out. At the same time the thought of keeping up this routine and the new appearance she would have if she used the make-up daily disturbed her a little. It was discreet, yes, she had told the girl that she must not look too made-up in her profession, but the change in her appearance would be noticed by some of her colleagues she was certain. The shampoos too worried her a little. They were to be used once a week, but would her hair fall back into it's style as the girl had predicted? She had suggested a weekly shampoo and set at Antoinette's, but at those prices it would be impossible. However, Carmichael had made an appointment for a further trim in six weeks' time.

She was still slightly bemused and surprised at her appearance when she had eventually had the temerity to open her eyes and look into the mirror, after the facial, the hair-do, the make-up and the eyebrow plucking. What had she seen? Carmichael, yes, still the long nose but somehow made to look

55

shorter, the reddened tip no longer red, the hair soft and gently waved round her face, the straggly pieces at the back which she could never manage now fitting perfectly into the nape of her neck as she could see when the girl, Janine, put the mirror behind her with a satisfied smirk. Carmichael could hardly believe it. The blusher so carefully applied high up on her cheek bones made her face more animated, gave it a more lifted look. The lipstick the girl had chosen was also discreet and the colour was outlined with a lip-brush – one of those was in the bag she carried – and then filled in to make the lips look fuller. It was a transformation which Carmichael could hardly believe. She was also scented rather too much for her own liking. She had tried various perfumes on her wrists before she had at last picked one, but it in no way resembled the perfume she had bought when she was going out with Harry and Emily. It was more elusive, more – she hesitated to use the word – more sophisticated.

She walked out of Antoinette's almost in a dream. She knew she would reproach herself later about the amount of money she had spent the more she thought about it, but at that moment her sense of well-being was such that she felt as if she was walking on air. If this was what it did to you no wonder the young girls gave doctors those long, sensual looks through their mascaraed eyelashes. She knew that she had mascara on and blinked rapidly. She had not noticed it, so skilfully had it been applied. But then the young girls, her young nurses, did not all wear mascara, it was the freshness and the youth of their faces – Carmichael dismissed that thought. When you were older you needed make-up. Where was it she had read – in a magazine probably – 'It is a brave woman who thinks she can do without make-up'? Well, she knew she had read that somewhere and here she was not only agreeing with but practising the idea.

Carmichael walked on firmly down the street, her head held high. There was no wind, not even a slight breeze to ruffle her hair, through she had a nasty feeling that, as usual, the beautiful set would not hold up in even a slight breeze or a spatter of rain. Still, she walked on hoping that the way the girl had cut her hair would do something to keep it in the same shape tomorrow as it was now. She glanced sideways at herself in a shop window and smiled complacently. She wondered if she dare wear this much make-up on duty and decided that, yes, she would. She had told the girl frankly what she did for a living and the young woman had understood perfectly.

'Oh, of course, Miss Carmichael, I will make it discreet, but then most make-up should be discreet, unless one is very young of course and uses these outrageous . . .' For once the reference to age had not hurt Carmichael.

Half-way down the street she was debating whether or not to go and have tea and wondering if it would ruin her lipstick. When she turned, preparing to cross the road, a man's voice said from behind her: 'Oh, er, Miss Carmichael, isn't it? Sister Carmichael? I didn't expect to see you out this sunny day, are you playing truant from the hospital?'

She turned and there stood the fire officer, Derek Hanson.

'Mr Hanson,' she said, trying not to simper in her usual manner. 'Yes, we both seem to be forgetting the hospital for a time.' It was a lame and silly answer but for the moment she could think of no other. The last person she had expected to see was the man who lately had been figuring so largely in her thoughts. It was very strange, fate perhaps? In rather an inexpert way she had been wondering how to set her cap at this man, or at least try, and here he was, appearing in the middle of the street when she was looking her best. It was quite, quite strange. Carmichael felt her heart beating a little faster, with pleasure this time, not with the usual anger or fear or resentment. It was almost worth the money she had spent in the shop to see the appreciation, the admiration, on his face.

'If I may say so on such a short aquaintance, you are looking most glamorous. May I say that without offending you?'

Carmichael shook her head. 'You don't offend me at all. It's very nice of you. I have just been to my beauty parlour,' She said this self-consciously.

Derek Hanson shook his head with a wry smile. 'Costly places these beauty parlours, costly places, but no doubt worth it, no doubt at all, very well-spent money.' He looked at her and Carmichael was not sure whether what he had said was the right thing, or whether this man would know, as Harry Maitland had known, the right and gentlemanly thing to say.

For the moment, however, she felt it was sufficient for her. She started out along the pavement again, forgetting that she had meant to cross the road, and Derek Hanson walked beside her.

'I've just taken my car to be serviced, such a nuisance. I have to get a bus back to the hospital. That's the trouble having these big hospitals in outlying places, if you haven't got a car you're stuck.'

Fate again, Carmichael wondered. Dear, dear fate. 'Are you going back to the hospital now? Do let me run you back, my car is just around the corner in the car-park.'

'That's very civil of you, Sister Carmichael, I certainly would be most grateful. I have an appointment at the hospital later on. Innumerable committees, endless talks we seem to be having to get this fire risk business straightened out, but no doubt it will all be worth it in the end.'

'I am sure it will,' said Carmichael, admitting to herself that this was a change of heart; now it seemed to her the most sensible appointment possible, though she remembered not so very long ago saying to someone that she didn't see why they'd appointed a fire officer.

They walked on in silence, and as they crossed the road to the car-park Derek Hanson put his hand gently under Carmichael's elbow to guide her through the traffic. She felt a thrill not only from the physical contact but from the fact that a man was walking along the road with her, looking after her, playing the male to her female. That was what she wanted, that was the next thing she had to learn, the appropriate reaction, what to say in order to hold, to amuse, to create admiration. 'Love begins at forty' – the phrase sprang into her mind and she felt herself blushing.

They arrived at the car-park and she unlocked her car. As Derek Hanson got in, he turned to her and smiled. Carmichael smiled back and with difficulty overcame her shyness and kept her eyes fixed on his face.

'If I may say so, the perfume you chose is quite breathtaking,' said Hanson, his brown eyes looking at her with complete concentration.

Carmichael who, she was aware, had thought his eyes hard before, now thought they were soft, manly, gentle.

'I'm afraid it's the combination of rather a lot of perfumes. I wanted a new one and I've been trying out several, you try them on your wrists, you know. I have chosen something a little more, well, a little more unusual than the others.'

She drove expertly to Hemmington General Hospital and stopped at the front door.

'Do you want to get out here, Mr Hanson?' she asked.

Derek Hanson was profuse in his thanks.

'Thank you so much, Sister Carmichael, thank you again. I wouldn't have managed to get back to the hospital for ages and I would have been late for my meeting. That's not good is it, not when you're first appointed?' He shook his head, smiling, and Carmichael agreed with him.

She wondered if she should ask him if she could run him out to fetch his car in her off-duty time the next day, but decided that that might be pushing it too much. She wasn't quite sure how she should behave. Should she be casual, would this man think she was after him? Yes, she decided, he probably would, so she said nothing and his next remark made her glad of her decision.

'The garage are bringing my car out to me which is very good of them, but they're always kind to hospital personnel, do you find that?' He showed no inclination to get out of the car and Carmichael relaxed a little and switched off her engine.

'Yes I do, I find they're very kind indeed. I use Jackson's Garage, is that where you've taken your car?'

He nodded. 'That's the one, nice crowd. They said they serviced quite a few hospital cars. Well . . .' He put his hand on the door and Carmichael felt her heart sink. Should she say something to delay him? Suddenly he turned back toward her.

'Miss Carmichael, I wonder if you would think me very pushy if I said I'd love to know which perfume you had chosen?' He laughed quite charmingly. 'No, I'm only using that as an excuse. I would be very pleased if you would have dinner with me one night. Do you think . . .?'

Carmichael found herself blushing and hated herself. She hoped he wouldn't notice and that the make-up the girl had put on would cover it.

'That would be very pleasant,' she said and felt like an old maid at the stilted reply.

'What night shall we say?'

Carmichael thought – or pretended to think.

'I'm not quite sure, this week is rather full. Next week I'd be delighted.' It was already Thursday so she felt she was not putting him off for too long.

'How about Tuesday? That would be all right for me if it would suit you.'

Carmichael thought again for a moment or two, thought of her blank diary, then said: 'I think Tuesday is all right. Yes, that will be fine.'

'I shall look forward to it,' said Derek Hanson and suddenly took her hand from the wheel and kissed it.

It was, Carmichael thought, an outrageous gesture from a man who had only just met her, once in the hospital and once in the street. Should she look outraged? But no, his smoothness disarmed her.

'Forgive me,' he said. 'It was the perfume, it really is quite overpowering in your car. You look so . . . well, please forgive a mere male.'

Carmichael looked down at the steering wheel and then back at him.

'Very well, Mr Hanson, I'll forgive you,' she said, trying to make her voice sound not too cool and not too coy. How did girls – women – manage, she thought almost in despair. How did one behave in a situation like this when a man whom one hardly knew kissed one's hand? She had no time to say anything before her companion continued: 'Derek, please. And your first name? We can't go out to dinner, can we, as Mr Hanson and Sister Carmichael?' By this time he was out of the car and was about to close the door. He looked at her quizzically.

'Agnes,' Carmichael said. She tried to sound demure and yet mature. He closed the door of the car, stood back, waved a hand and waited for her to drive away. That Carmichael appreciated, that she knew to be good manners.

She drove the short distance to the nurses' home, trembling with unfamiliar pleasure. It had been wonderful having a man in the car beside her. She'd only given him a lift but it would be wonderful going out to dinner with him in his car. After all, even with Harry, Emily had driven. This would be different. He would be looking after her for the evening. He would be taking her to dinner, asking what she would like to eat, where she would like to sit. She felt younger, prettier and almost desirable – but running through this feeling was a slight thin thread of fear.

10

In spite of everything, Auxiliary Nurse Debbie Pearson seemed happy enough in Casualty much to Carmichael's regret. She would have liked Pearson to ask for a transfer back to a ward, but she suspected from a few remarks she had heard from the other sisters that the auxiliary had been none too popular in any of the wards in which she had worked. Her insolence did not disappear despite Carmichael's cold handling and threats to report her. She seemed utterly without fear of the management, or of being reported to the nursing officer, or even being sacked. Not without a certain amount of envy Carmichael thought that the woman just didn't care for anyone or anybody. Flaunting her bouncy little body round the department, she would glance sideways, through the lashes that Carmichael always suspected were false, at the doctors and porters, indeed at any man, and what was more the men responded, almost all of them. They liked her, Carmichael felt with contempt, they liked her. They didn't seem to take any notice of the fact that she was an extremely bad nurse and a very common woman.

Carmichael felt strongly about this. Pearson was a bad nurse and Carmichael had once or twice caught her yanking a child to the theatre when the mother was too frightened to go in to see the child sutured. Carmichael always encouraged mothers or fathers to go into the theatre with their children so that the offspring would not feel deprived. It was one of Carmichael's 'things'. She liked to think that the parents thought well of her, but she had seen Pearson, if a mother cringed, pulling the child by the arm and saying brusquely: 'Come on then, you silly child, and stop yelling.' Admittedly this was after she was out of earshot of the mother, but she was rarely out of hearing of the ever-pricked ears of her senior sister.

'That is not the way to speak to a patient even if it is a child, Nurse Pearson,' she had said on more than one occasion.

Nurse Pearson usually replied sullenly: 'Well, the mother is too daft to come in and the child won't stop yelling.'

Each time Carmichael had taken the child away from Nurse Pearson and given it to another nurse to look after or else had done so herself. Each time she had chalked it up against the auxiliary nurse. She had never caught her in actual cruelty, not as yet. Then one morning she did catch her being unpleasantly callous with a patient. This was enough for Carmichael and she would have thought enough for Debbie Pearson's downfall.

It happened one morning when they were rather busy. An old lady had been brought in with a very badly scalded hand. She had been warming some shoe polish under the grill. The shoe polish had been very old, she informed the nurse, and she didn't want to waste it. She thought if she put it under the grill it would soften, but when she had come to remove the tin, the polish, now fairly hot, had spilled on to her fingers giving her a nasty scald and her neighbour had insisted, quite rightly, that she came to the Casualty department.

The clerk had taken her particulars and she had come straight through into a dressing room. Carmichael had been fairly busy at the time with various casualties but she noted out of the corner of her eye that the old lady was being hustled by Nurse Pearson into the cubicle. Then she had momentarily put the matter to one side in her mind while she dealt with what she felt were more urgent cases. With her usual flouncing walk Pearson came out to look at the clerk's card, made a face and then went up to one of the doctors and said flippantly in Carmichael's hearing: 'Silly old bitch in there has poured shoe polish over her hand. Can you imagine! It must have been boiling hot. I don't know what to do, you'd better see it before I start to clean it up.'

Carmichael immediately intervened. 'It is not your business to do anything, whatever doctor says. Let a staff nurse see it, Nurse Pearson.' She said it so coldly and bluntly that the woman turned to her with her usual wide-eyed look.

'OK, Sister. I don't want to put my nose in where it's not

63

wanted. I just thought I'd tell the doctor, that's all.'

The doctor nodded absently and said: 'I'll be with her in a moment, but I must cope with this kid who's got a fish-hook in his finger and is yelling blue murder.' He disappeared into a cubicle.

Carmichael finished what she was doing and then made her way to the old lady's examination room.

Nurse Pearson should not have left her; she should have waited for a staff nurse, got the patient on the couch and let her lie down. Carmichael went into the examination cubicle and was horrified. The old lady had pitched forward out of the chair on to the floor and lay there, apparently unconscious, bleeding from the side of her forehead where she'd hit the floor. Carmichael put her head round the curtains of the examination room and called the doctor. The urgency of her tone made him come at once.

'What's happened?' he asked as he came in. Then he saw the unconscious woman. 'Oh Lord, has she fainted?'

'She shouldn't have been left, she's cut her head. Look'. The hand which had been covered with a green towel was now exposed; it showed a nasty scald covered with brown shoe polish.

'What the hell has she been doing to her hand?' said the doctor, rather testily, presumably, Carmichael supposed, because he was so busy. Usually he was a patient young man. Carmichael went out and came back within seconds with the card.

'She was warming shoe polish under the grill and it went over her hand. Not a very sensible thing to do perhaps, but after all she looks very elderly.' Then her eye caught the name at the top of the casualty card, 'Lady Thornton,' she said. 'Lady Thornton. Well, Nurse Pearson might at least have told me.'

'Why, does having a title make any difference?' said the doctor wryly. He lifted the patient bodily and laid her on the couch. They could now see that she'd bruised her eye as well. She began to recover consciousness and rocked her head to and fro.

'No, it doesn't make any difference. All patients are treated the same, but you never know with titled people. They are

64

often friends of friends in the hospital hierarchy. Anyway, it's not good for the department whoever she is.'

Carmichael called in a senior nurse and together they began to bathe the woman's forehead.

The doctor placed the hand on a sterile towel and said: 'Get a trolley, please.' The nurse complied and he very gingerly started to take the polish out of the scalded area. It came off in greasy layers showing red, bare flesh.

'Nasty,' he said. He looked up at the old lady now gazing at him with astonishment. She uttered the usual 'Where am I?'

Carmichael continued bathing her forehead and said gently: 'Don't worry, Lady Thornton, you're all right. You've scalded your hand.'

'I know I have, but my head hurts,' the old lady said looking at her accusingly.

'Yes, you had a little fall too,' said Carmichael, and the doctor raised his eyes heavenward and went on working on the hand.

Carmichael continued to bathe the injured forehead and eye, noting that it would want at least two stitches. The eye was closing a little but otherwise seemed uninjured, just a bruise, she thought. How was she going to explain, who should she tell? First she'd have a word with Nurse Pearson.

The senior nurse and doctor continued administering to the old lady and Carmichael, seething with rage, went out of the examination room and into the main part of Casualty. Nurse Pearson was just going by with a trolley.

'Come with me to my office at once,' said Carmichael.

'Staff nurse wants this . . .' Nurse Pearson answered pertly.

'Wheel it in to her, then follow me,' said Sister Carmichael.

The woman did so, making a clatter that was totally unnecessary. When she arrived in Carmichael's office Carmichael closed the door. She did not ask Nurse Pearson to sit down.

'You left a patient unattended and that patient collapsed on the floor and injured her head. She has cut it and it will need suturing. You must know the consequences of this, nurse, it is flagrant negligence. You know perfectly well that you should never leave a patient alone, particularly one of her age, when she first enters the department. You should have asked for help, got her to lie down on the couch and then stayed with her until a senior nurse or myself had taken over. She is a very old lady, a very old lady indeed. Why did you act as you did?'

The reply startled Carmichael.

'Well, her and her title – Lady Thornton – I thought she could wait a bit. I mean, why isn't she private? I expect she thinks she should have more attention than anyone else. I just sat her down, after all it was only her hand.'

'She is eighty-four and probably quite poor by the look of her clothes,' said Carmichael. She was still enraged, but very controlled. This could easily cause trouble for her department, the accusation of having neglected or even been cruel towards a patient. To leave her, a shaky old lady hardly able to walk. Carmichael had seen that, she'd been brought in by the ambulance people in a wheelchair and after that she'd been almost roughly handled by her nurse, a nurse for whom she, Sister Carmichael, was responsible.

'I shall report you, of course, to Miss Thompson. Where the complaint will go from there I have no idea. The patient herself may bring a complaint. She's already coming round and realizing that she was left and that she fell. It might well affect your nursing career.'

'I don't care if it does. What kind of career have I got?' Nurse Pearson stuck her lower lip out, but Carmichael noticed it was trembling and hoped that perhaps the nurse was more affected by what had happened than she seemed to be.

'Your conduct towards patients leaves a lot to be desired. I have noticed it the whole time you have been here in Casualty. I don't think that you are suitable for nursing in this department or indeed for nursing at all in any capacity.'

'Other reports on the wards have always been all right, I've never had . . .'

'That is not true. You know perfectly well that on the geriatric ward you were reprimanded for roughly handling an old lady who was trying to get back into bed after you had taken her to the bath. I'm well aware of these things, you know. You yourself read the report before you signed it, so now you are merely lying.' Carmichael rose, she felt she had said enough.

'Is the old lady all right?' asked Nurse Pearson.

Carmichael looked at her long and reprovingly.

'The doctor is with her, we shall see. She may well have to be admitted because of her fall, not because of her burnt hand. I would have thought you have enough experience to be left to take a patient into an examination room. I would not have thought the responsibility was too great, but obviously it was.'

'I didn't mean it, Sister, I was just a bit hurried.'

'You were not a bit hurried, you had plenty of time. Your action was like many of your other actions, cruel and thoughtless. Now please return to your duties and keep away from patients, merely clean up after the other nurses.'

Nurse Pearson's face was a deep scarlet. Carmichael walked out of her office and the girl followed her but Carmichael did not look at her again. She went back into the dressing room to see Lady Thornton who was still slightly bewildered by her fall. When it was suggested by the doctor that she be admitted to the ward she acquiesced.

'Do you live alone, Lady Thornton?' Carmichael asked. She found herself liking using the title and she wondered if perhaps she herself was a slight snob and Nurse Pearson was an inverted one.

The old lady nodded.

'Yes I do, I live absolutely alone. I've got a budgie but my next-door neighbour would look after him if you would telephone her.' She opened her handbag, old and scuffed, but a real leather one Carmichael noticed, and took out a piece of paper on which was written the neighbour's number.

At least she's not confused after the fall, thought Carmichael gratefully, but it had got to be reported nevertheless to her nursing officer. She dreaded doing it; that anything so very inefficient had happened in her department made her feel physically sick.

She hoped Miss Thompson would deal adequately with Debbie Pearson, get her dismissed if possible, but in her heart she knew this was unlikely. In her opinion Miss Thompson pandered to the nurses. She would call this 'just a slight problem'. It was all untrue that the nurse had been overworked or rushed, but the nursing officer did not like rocking the boat in any of the wards or departments of which she was in charge. She would not make much of it and the girl would be allowed to go on being nasty to patients. Yes, nasty, because she was a nasty woman and Carmichael vowed that life in Casualty would not be pleasant for her. Nurse Pearson would regret the fact that she had given Casualty a black mark, unless of course Miss Thompson decided to move her. Then she would go to a ward and go on being as unpleasant to patients as she was here. She rang the ward to which Lady Thornton was to be admitted.

The immediate reaction was, 'Lady Thornton? Can't she go in the private wing?'

'No, she can't, everyone with a title isn't rich, you know,' said Carmichael briskly. 'She's got a nasty burn on her hand and unfortunately while she was here in Casualty she had a fall. We've had to stitch her forehead and her eye is badly bruised. She fell forwards out of a chair.' Carmichael felt it was better to tell the ward herself before Lady Thornton did.

'Why the hell wasn't someone looking after her then?'

The sister of the orthopaedic ward did not want to take an old lady with a burned hand and injured head. She had more important things on her ward like hips and knees that had been operated on. Carmichael knew the feeling. She herself had had an orthopaedic ward but sister would have to take the old woman and Carmichael said so, coldly. There was no love lost between her and this particular sister. Grumbling, the ward sister acquiesced and put the phone down with a bit of a bang. Patients seem to come last, said Carmichael under her breath as she walked out of her office.

The old lady was still lying with eyes closed although she opened them immediately Carmichael went in.

'We'll take you up to the ward, just for observation, just for a night or maybe two.'

'All right, Sister, I understand perfectly and I'll be very glad to be in for a couple of nights. Will you phone that number for me about the budgie? I mean I wouldn't like him to starve.'

Carmichael, her voice more gentle than usual said: 'Of course, I'll do it now. Has she got a key to get into your . . .' she looked at the casualty card, then went on, '. . . into your flat?'

Lady Thornton nodded. 'Yes, she has. She can get in all right and she knows where the seed and things are, she'll do it properly, she's done it before.' She sounded suddenly weary and Carmichael felt a stab of fear. The fall might have done more damage than appeared.

She turned to the young doctor and said in a very low voice so that Lady Thornton couldn't hear: 'Do you think we should have an X-ray, of her skull I mean?'

He nodded in a business-like way. 'I'll write the form out, just to cover ourselves,' he said in an equally low voice. He went towards the doctors' office to fill in the X-ray form.

Carmichael called the staff nurse in, and explained the situation rapidly and softly. The staff nurse looked slightly worried – as well she might, thought Carmichael.

Carmichael laid her hand gently on Lady Thornton's arm, avoiding the bandaged hand.

'I'll ring for a porter and you can go to X-ray with her,' she said to her staff nurse. Then, to Lady Thornton: 'You're just going to have an X-ray and I've told the ward you're coming so they'll be expecting you.' As she went out of the dressing room and crossed over to another room where a new patient had just been moved in, she came face to face with Nurse Pearson. Pearson's face was still red and her eyes looked swollen. She was wheeling a trolley, and blood on the instruments showed that it had been used.

'Cover that up. You don't want patients seeing things like that,' said Carmichael.

The girl raised her eyes, and there was hatred in them. Carmichael thought that she had been crying.

'All right, Sister,' she said and flapped the sides of the green towel over the blood-stained instruments. They were still not quite covered so she took a disposable towel and plonked it heavily on the top of the trolley.

Carmichael walked with a stiff back towards her office. She would have her coffee now, everything was under control. Whatever happened to Nurse Pearson, whether she stayed or left, Carmichael would see to it that she took no more responsibility in this department, and if Miss Thompson saw fit to move her to a ward, she would warn the sister of that ward exactly what the girl was like.

11

Each morning Carmichael carefully applied her lipstick as she had been taught by the girl at Antoinette's. It seemed to disappear quickly from her lips and she had trouble with the outline – she felt that, unlike most other people, her lips ran into the skin of her face and the outline, when painted on, looked nice but not stable. Each morning she got up early and made up her face in the hope that Derek Hanson would come to her department, but he did not. She had not seen him.

She sat down in her chair and looked at herself and thought, is it worth it? Yes, she decided. There was the dinner to look forward to, even if she didn't see him before. Whenever she looked at her face she seemed to think of him.

Then one morning she looked up through the glass of her office and saw him approaching the nursing station, walking between the examination rooms. She noticed again the rather military swagger of his walk. How strange, one moment he was in her thoughts and then suddenly there he was. She stood up hastily, felt her face flushing and wondered what she would say to him; then she thought, I'll just look at him and leave the first remark to him. She was thankful that she had put on the perfume which she used so sparingly in the morning, and as she stirred she could smell it and hoped he would too. He came closer, then, smiling, entered her office.

'Good morning, Sister Carmichael,' he said.

Carmichael almost fluttered. She stepped forward, keeping her eyes determinedly fixed on his. He smiled again and there was something between them that Carmichael had seen between others but never experienced herself – a sensuality, a sexual awareness? He put out a hand but she was too shy to

70

take it. Pretending not to notice his extended hand, she turned and saw that Nurse Pearson had dumped her trolley and was coming back this way, passing the nursing station and Carmichael's office. Pearson was watching as if she had sized up the situation between Carmichael and Derek Hanson at a glance. Carmichael could almost hear her say: 'After him is she? Fat chance she's got.' A malicious little smile played on the girl's face as she walked by.

Carmichael noticed with dismay that Derek Hanson's eyes were following the girl, watching the fat little bottom twitch as she moved away. He turned back to Carmichael almost at once and smiled again warmly, 'See you on Tuesday evening. I'm so looking forward to it,' he said and Carmichael nodded, reassured.

During the time between Derek Hanson's visit to her department and the Tuesday they were to dine together, Carmichael was conscious of a curious change in her attitude – at least, she found it curious. She was just as meticulous in the department, just as demanding of her nurses, just as solicitous for her patients – that all remained unchanged – but at the back of her mind she saw a new future for herself, a future side by side with a man who would be concerned for her welfare, who would live his life with her, be part of her life. These thoughts brought about a change in her feelings towards the young nurses when she saw them glance at the doctors or the porters. It made her feel more tolerant, more secure, feel that she was, in a way, one of them.

Carmichael was quite honest in thinking that had she been pretty and desirable she might not have chosen Derek Hanson. He was not, her mind said, in her class – yet in another way he was, for what was she? Nothing. Her one disastrous love affair – and she called it that, not associating it in any way with her feelings towards Derek – had been her relationship with Harry, Professor Maitland, and he had been on an intellectual level that had been above her. No, she would have to be satisfied with this man, this fire officer. Well, she might even continue her job when they were married, but she could think about that later. It was not that that she wished for, it was to be able to refer to 'my husband' and to know that he referred to her as 'my

71

wife'. That was what she wanted most: someone who was intimately concerned with everything she did and everything that happened to her and would, presumably, care whether she was happy or sad.

Almost without realizing it she shied away from the side of marriage which she was not sure about, the sexual side, the house-keeping side, the living intimately with a man, sharing the bathroom, sharing everything. She was vaguely aware, although she shied away from these things, that that was really what she wanted: not to be alone, not to go on holiday alone, not to watch television alone – anything to escape from living the next half of her life in loneliness.

She marvelled a little at her own mixed feelings. Although she had been conscious of the loneliness before, it had never assumed such importance as now, for meeting this man had accentuated it. She felt she could not bear to spend the rest of her life going back to a nurses' home and later perhaps to another cottage of her own. It would not suffice. There would have to be someone else to tell things to when she came home and who in turn would be able to tell her things. Little sentences formed in her mind like, 'What kind of day have you had, dear?' 'Have you been busy today?' 'Were the people at the hospital cooperative?' Yet she was not in love, the feeling she had for Derek Hanson was nothing like the feeling she had had for Harry. She smiled to herself. Was she making this out of nothing, manufacturing it for her own convenience? Perhaps she was. Perhaps she'd wanted this all along, just this companionship. She was not altogether sure. Years ago it had been promotion she had wanted; she felt even now that had she been able to achieve the post of chief nursing officer, as had once been her ambition, Derek Hanson would have had no part to play in her life. Now that was all changed, and her make-up, her hair, everything was geared towards the only man who had appeared on her horizon who was even slightly suitable in age and, she had to admit it, of some kind of mental equality to herself.

These thoughts were a sort of constant back-drop to Carmichael's days and nights. Wherever she went in the hospital – to the dining room, to the pathological laboratory or to X-ray, anywhere – she looked for him, hoping to meet him, but she seldom saw him. Then, again, somehow that did not matter. It was a large hospital and the thought that he might be dating someone else didn't enter her head. She felt that for some reason he was, to put it crudely, after her, but with her usual honesty, as she looked at herself in the mirror, she wondered why. But it did not matter as long as they married – marriage, nothing else, was her goal. She had to admit to herself, too, that knowing that he was there in the hospital somewhere, although she did not see him, was satisfying.

The Tuesday dinner was an unqualified success. Carmichael made herself up with extra care, not quite so discreetly as she did when working in the Casualty department. She put on a little more eyeshadow, a little more lipstick and a tiny bit more rouge. She was satisfied with her appearance. Her dress, everything about her looked attractive – as attractive, that is, as she could make herself. She knew that the red tip of her nose would probably show through her make-up before the evening was over, but she could repair it. Her hair might not stand up to the evening but at the moment it looked fine. She packed her evening bag carefully with the cosmetics she thought she might need. A touch of her perfume, a tiny bit more than usual, and she was ready.

Derek Hanson arrived on time. He was wearing a dark, well-cut suit and a tie emblazoned with a small gold motif. He looked very presentable; more than that, he looked handsome. The wave in his hair was slightly deeper than Carmichael had noticed before, as if he had pressed it in carefully with his hand. He was vain, thought Carmichael automatically, without being unduly critical.

When she stepped into the car the feeling swelled in her that this, this was it: to be driven, to have your man take you out, to have your man treat you in a manner that was both familiar and yet fond. She had seen intimate looks pass between husband and wife, between boyfriend and girlfriend, and it was now possible for her too. It would take time, of course, and for the moment she sat almost primly beside Derek in the car. He had remarked on her perfume and appearance and this had pleased her.

At dinner he talked perhaps too much about himself but she listened with her eyes fixed determinedly on his, hoping desperately all the time that her make-up was standing up to the food and drink and that her lipstick had not smudged or entirely disappeared.

It was inevitable, Carmichael thought, that she should compare him with Harry Maitland. Derek's manner on arrival at the table which he had booked, was slightly ostentatious, his attitude to the waiter rather too matey. Though Carmichael's experience had been limited to Emily and Harry Maitland, hospital dinners and the occasional consultant's cocktail party, she was perceptive enough to notice that his voice was a shade too loud, that he wished to show her and those at adjacent tables that he knew his way around the wine list. As Carmichael sat quietly listening to him she set these down as marks against him, but then again there were his punctuality, his attentiveness and his open-handedness at the bar before they sat down at the table. All this had surprised her, and his 'Have one yourself?' had obviously pleased the barman whose 'Thank you, sir' had equally gratified Derek. There were faults, yes, but then there were faults within herself and Carmichael was willing to overlook almost anything.

The wine, the food and the warmth made Carmichael glow, feel mellow and less anxious and she let his voice wash over her, attending to the long monologue with only half her mind, occasionally saying, 'Really' or 'How very sad' as the occasion arose, while the other half of her mind was acutely assessing his eligibility, and finding that her resolution remained unchanged.

He had lost his wife, he told her, years ago, in childbirth. The child too had died and he'd never recovered from it, it had been a dreadful blow. He dropped his eyes for a moment and played with the stem of his wineglass, but Carmichael felt nothing, no pity for him – only slight interest. This, she thought to herself wryly, is not love on my part and she remembered Harry again and the terrible feeling of pity for his blindness, but here with this man – well, she must dismiss the thought of Harry and concentrate on Derek who was now telling her of his life in the army and afterwards in the fire service and the lonely life he led now in a bachelor flat. He had always wanted, he told her, a cottage in the country, to grow his own flowers and vegetables, but what was the use of doing that alone, where was the joy in that? Carmichael dragged her mind back from her reverie to voice her agreement with him.

'And you have never met anyone to share your life with?' It was a bold and rather uncharacteristic remark but with Derek she felt she could ask such an intimate question. After all he had asked her . . .

He glanced up at her quickly and some of the gloom on his face vanished.

'No, no I haven't,' he said. 'I have never found what in romantic books I believe is called "Mrs Right".'

Carmichael replied archly: 'I thought it was the woman who had to find "Mr Right" not the man find "Mrs . . ."' They both laughed, rather stiltedly, uncomfortably.

'Perhaps that is so, I haven't read many romantic novels,' Derek said and Carmichael did not confess that when she was young she had devoured them. She thought as she gazed at him how unlike this grey-haired man was to the tall, muscular, dark-haired men of the love stories, usually called Garth or Trevelyan, and she smiled a secret smile at the thought of them and wondered when he would stop talking about himself and ask about her. Still, one must be a good listener, that much she had learned from romantic novels, so she sat quietly, listening to him droning on about what he had wanted and how he had been unable to achieve it so far.

At last, when they were sipping the liqueurs that he insisted they should have, he suddenly stopped talking about himself and said, 'Now what about you, what about you, Agnes? You've been listening to me right through dinner, so now please tell me about yourself.'

Carmichael did so. She found it pleasant to talk to someone who was really interested. She told him about her cottage, about the vandalism, about her changing nursing posts – not a word of course about the fact that she had been unable to obtain promotion, not a word about Harry, not a word about the psychiatric hospital, or the orphanage were she had been raised. Carmichael told him just what she wanted him to know and he listened with sympathy and concern.

'And why have you remained unmarried? An attractive girl like you, have you never found anybody? I don't understand why a girl like you should remain single.'

Carmichael dropped her eyes and perhaps the animated expression on her face changed, for he put his hand across the table and covered hers and said: 'Perhaps, like me, you've never found the really right person. And now you must miss your cottage. Have you let it to someone?'

Carmichael looked up quickly. 'Oh no, I sold it,' she said. Then in a rush of confidence she went on: 'I got a good deal more money for it than I paid, which was all to the good. One day I hope to buy another cottage, a bigger one, when I'm more settled. I just don't know. The nurses' home at the moment is comfortable but . . .' she left the rest unsaid and Derek seemed to understand.

'Yes, you're right. I'm sure the nurses' home is quite comfortable, I did a tour round it for the fire inspection, you know. It's well appointed.'

'It is,' Carmichael answered and for a moment their eyes met and locked. Carmichael felt her lids redden, her face flush and she rose abruptly saying, 'Excuse me, I must go to the powder room.'

As she rose to her feet her evening bag fell to the floor. With an exaggerated flourish Derek Hanson immediately got up, came round to her side of the table, picked up the bag from the floor and handed it to her. She took the bag from his hand irritably.

She stood in front of the mirror in the ladies' room, under the bright light above it, her hands on the wash basin in front of her. She felt hot, uncomfortable and unreal. Perhaps it was the wine and liqueur. Where was this all getting her, where was she going to? She felt as if she were on some kind of slide, slipping, slipping into another life she was not sure she could handle – life with a man. Wouldn't it be better to do as she had said at the table, get herself a little cottage somewhere near this great big hospital and prepare for retirement, maybe get more pets? Then she shook herself. That would mean every night going home from work to a lonely cottage, getting her supper as she had in the last cottage. Her life was not going to be like that, she would not let it. You must take risks, everybody who married took a risk, of course they did, they didn't really know how it was going to turn out. Her devotion to nursing was wavering, she felt, wavering as promotion disappeared into the distance. She would always like nursing, but nursing was not enough. not now.

She powdered the end of her nose, reapplied her lipstick and almost marched back to the dining room. She held her shoulders straight and stiff and there was determination on her face. She saw Derek Hanson look at her in a rather puzzled way as if he noticed the change in her, a change from the acquiescent, pliant Carmichael who had listened to him and told him about herself to the stiff-backed woman who now sat down again at his table.

They drove home in silence. She wondered if she had done something wrong, put him off by her attitude when she had returned from the ladies' room, perhaps she had said something another woman would not have done. But it seemed not, for as they arrived and he drew the car to a standstill at the nurses' home door, she felt a momentary panic as he switched off the engine and turned to her, undoing his seat belt and putting his arm along the back of her seat.

He did not at first touch her shoulder. Perhaps he could sense her rigidity because he said suddenly, softly, and to Carmichael completely in character: 'I would like to kiss you, your perfume is certainly . . .' He smiled.

Carmichael turned towards him and realized it was not his mouth she was thinking of but of her lipstick. She let him kiss her and noticed that the lipstick did leave a slight crooked imprint on his mouth. It was not romantic and she did nothing about it. In some of the stories she had read the girl would have taken out a perfumed handkerchief and wiped the man's lips, or even have done so with her thumb but Carmichael could not do that, could not bring herself to touch his mouth with her hand and for some reason she shuddered, a fact which Derek Hanson seemed not to notice.

'When can I see you again, Agnes?' he said.

'I'm off early on Friday.' Carmichael's voice trembled and she saw a slight smile form on Derek Hanson's lips. She wondered if she had said what the other nurses would have said. Was she being too eager? Had the fact that she had shivered suddenly made him mistake it for . . .? Was that quite what he expected? Did that slight quiver in her voice make him think she found him irresistible sexually?

He seemed satisfied and complacent and said: 'Friday, that would be great. What would you like to do, go to a movie, go for a drive, or what?'

'I don't mind,' said Carmichael, her primness had returned.

'Same time, same place?' he said almost gaily and she nodded; he got out of the car and went round to open the door for her.

'Good night, Agnes,' he said.

As Carmichael was about to reply, turning to walk up the steps to the door of the nurses' home, a man dashed out of the shrubbery in front of the car and for a moment showed up clearly in the headlights. Carmichael recognized him at once – it was the flasher, the same man she had seen through her window. His hair stood up round his face in spikes as if it was wet but this time he had on a collar and tie, the white shirt showing under his long overcoat. He sprinted up the drive and Derek Hanson slipped back into the driver's seat of the car, preparing to go after him, but this merely made the man run faster. It had probably frightened him, Carmichael thought, and that was a good thing, it might make him keep away from the place. Derek decided not to pursue him and Carmichael had to admit that it would have been useless, in no time at all he had completely disappeared.

'That's the bounder is it? That's the one you saw, do you think it's the same man?'

Carmichael nodded.

'I'll stop by the hospital and say he's around again, that I've seen him. I should lock your window, Agnes.' Derek Hanson got out of the car and stood looking up the driveway. Then he came round to her again, took hold of her arm and repeated fondly: 'Lock your window, Agnes.' A man's advice to a woman he cared about, that was how Carmichael read it and she felt warm.

'I will, it's locked now, at least I think it is. I'll be careful.'

She knew the window was locked but she wanted him to care, to think about it, to hope that she had locked it, that she remembered when she went in. The warm glow continued as Derek got into the car and she went through the doors into the home. He wanted to see her again on Friday, only three days away. She felt satisfied, happy. She put the key in her room door, went in and closed it behind her. She went over and tried the window. She was right, she had known she had locked it before she went out, but then she was always pretty meticulous in the things she did.

She caught a glimpse of herself in the mirror as she went by the dressing table. Her make-up had not stood up to the evening well in spite of touching it up in the ladies' room and her hair, instead of remaining neatly set and shining as it had when she had left the hairdresser had flopped and had sunk down on her head in its usual thin, scrappy manner. But did it matter? She looked better than she used to. Perhaps she should try to put on more weight, men did like plumper women, but she balked at that thought. Having Derek Hanson for her own meant someone to open car doors for her, someone to escort her, someone to talk about, an engagement ring maybe – but she didn't want to go any further in her thoughts than that. She ruled out all thoughts of intimacy, bed, sex, she didn't want to spoil the evening.

As she undressed and took off her make-up she suddenly thought of washing his shirts and socks. The idea did not particularly appeal to her, but, if she was going to be a wife, it would have to be done. I may have to go on working, I don't know, she thought, but in any event those things, those intimate things have got to be done. Carmichael sat with her chin in her hands and wondered if there was any other woman in the hospital thinking the same thoughts as she was at this moment? It must occur to women that they would have to do a great many things – that they wouldn't be living for themselves any more, when they thought of marriage. She wondered if other women worried and wished that she was able to talk about this to someone.

Derek Hanson was quite eligible, he was fifty or near it, and there were one or two sisters around her age who she was sure would . . . Her mouth straightened into a thin determined line. Well, if I can't have him, nobody else will, she thought and remembered again how he had watched Nurse Pearson's plump bottom. It no longer worried her. She felt as she usually did, that she could get what she wanted if she went the right way about it. She was not at the moment quite sure what the right way was, but again she said, this time aloud: 'If I can't have him nobody else will.' She said it to the image in the mirror.

It was certainly a new venture for her, she thought, something that would add zest to her life if she could get over the worry, in fact it would change it entirely. Then she wondered if she should buy more clothes for Friday. Should she spend more money? Perhaps she might get another dress, after all she had reason to dress well now. Her flagging spirits revived, life seemed quite different.

12

Next morning when Carmichael went on duty she was greeted at once by her senior staff nurse.

'That flasher has been seen again last night, Sister, you didn't see him, did you? Nurse Matthews did, she was frightened to death. He was dressed, though. At least, when he opened his overcoat he'd got clothes on underneath, but he exposed himself she said. It's awful, isn't it? I wish they'd catch him. I think it's too bad for these youngsters going home at night in the dark to be met by someone like that.'

'Why only for the youngsters?' said Carmichael. 'Yes, I did see him, my friend and I saw him. He blew his car horn and gave chase and tried to catch him, but the man raced away up the drive very quickly.' Carmichael said this selfconsciously. She wanted people, particulary her own nurses, to know that she had dates too like the rest of them. Derek certainly hadn't gone dashing up the drive but why not exaggerate a little.

'Well, I wouldn't tackle him. They're usually nasty, these people, he might carry a knife, Sister, you don't know. I wouldn't let my boyfriend go after him if he did see him, you never know, do you?' She had taken notice of Carmichael's remark and Carmichael felt pleased that her nurse had used the word 'boyfriend' in connection with herself, comparing, as it were, herself with Carmichael and without surprise, just taking it for granted that Carmichael should have been out with a man.

She went in search of Nurse Matthews who was in a cubicle bandaging a patient. Carmichael bent down to look critically at the bandage. It appeared to satisfy her. The man who was being tended rose to his feet and said: 'Shall I make an appointment for a week ahead then, nurse?' The nurse nodded to him and

81

the man walked out of the cubicle pushing aside the plastic curtain as he did so. The nurse tidied the curtain after him and looked towards Sister Carmichael.

'I hear you had an encounter with that awful man who is haunting the nurses' home. He was there last night again, Nurse Matthews.' Her voice was quite mellow and her manner less rigid than usual

'Yes, Sister, I did. He frightened me I can tell you. I walked down the drive, it was fairly light and then I saw him, he came round one of the corners of the nurses' home. He opened his coat and, well, it wasn't very nice. He was dressed though, not naked like he was when you saw him, that was something, I suppose. I know I screamed and someone came out of the nurses' home, another nurse, I didn't know her, well I'd seen her about but that's all. She was very nice, she made me go in and made me some tea. I wish they'd catch him. I shall ask my boyfriend to come all the way down the drive with me, I really will, but he was in a hurry last night, he'd got to meet someone. I'm not going down there alone again.'

Carmichael had to say it, she just had to repeat the remarks she had made to her senior staff nurse.

'Yes I know, my friend brought me home and we saw him, we saw him come round from one side near the door of the nurses' home and right across the lights of my boyfriend's car. He ran very fast up the drive. I was just telling staff nurse how my friend started to go after him but then decided against it. I was glad he didn't go. As I said, "What's the use? he might carry a knife." '

Carmichael knew she was talking too much to a junior nurse but the junior nurse showed no surprise that Carmichael had been out with a man and again Carmichael was pleased; she must broadcast it a bit to consolidate the relationship, she would let everyone know she was going out with Derek Hanson. After all, she wanted it known, it would make the position more stable. If it got back to him that she was talking about it, he would realize that she was expecting something of him. She wondered whether this was the right way to go about it or whether it would frighten him off. No, she decided, it would not and she thought she'd talk about it again when she went to

82

lunch with the other sisters.

Nigel Denton came down to the department in the morning and greeted her familiarly, more like an old friend. They discussed one or two cases that had been admitted from the department and Carmichael was delighted to think that he felt she would still be interested in cases which had left Casualty and gone to the wards. They also talked about the business of dressings and when to send the patients to their own doctors and when to get them treated outside by a district nurse. This was always a problem. Very often the patients preferred to come to Casualty, especially if they were old. They felt it was rather a treat to come to the hospital and talk to the nurses. But hospital cars and transport were difficult to arrange and if possible out-patients were unloaded on to their general practitioners' nurses. Even that was not easy for some of them, but then the business of transport became the doctor's responsibility and not the hospital's.

Nigel Denton asked her pleasantly if she'd send for some coffee and they'd have it together and then at last he began to talk about the old days.

Miss Creasey was mentioned, the Casualty officer at St Jude's, and Nigel Denton told her where Miss Creasey was now working. Carmichael blossomed under these memories although for her they were far from happy. Marion Hughes's death too came up, and Carmichael thought that Nigel Denton, as he sipped his coffee, was no doubt thinking of his own dead wife. She wondered whether the years that had passed had eased the problem. There was no smell of drink on his breath this morning and Carmichael was glad. She wanted everyone's happiness, she smiled to herself. She was doing a lot of smiling. Then she recounted the incident of the flasher to Nigel Denton and he looked at her with some concern.

'Bloody man,' he said. 'Why don't they manage to catch him? I wish they wouldn't bother so much about parked cars and catch someone like him. He'll frighten some of the kids to death, it's not good enough.'

Again Carmichael primly remarked that she had been out with her man friend but this time the reaction was different. Nigel Denton looked at her quizzically.

'Oh, so you're going to leave the ranks are you? Are you going to get married and disappear? Well, it will be a great loss though perhaps when you do get married you'll go on working?'

Carmichael felt the colour in her cheeks rise as usual but this time it was useful for Nigel Denton looked at her raised colour and laughed in a friendly way.

'Oh I can see there's something going on here,' he said and Carmichael actually laughed with embarrassment.

'Oh, come now, Mr Denton,' she said. 'We go out together but that doesn't mean . . . not yet anyway.'

'Who is the lucky man, do I know him?'

Carmichael told him and he nodded.

'Ah yes, I've heard about him. I haven't met him, though, he hasn't been here long, has he? Did you know him before, then? Before he came here?'

Carmichael was noncommittal, she didn't want him to know that she'd only been going out with Derek Hanson for such a short time.

'Yes, I can see, you knew him before.' Nigel Denton got up. 'I'm hoping to marry again, Sister,' he went on suddenly, his hands on the back of the chair. He looked at her as if he wasn't seeing her. 'I never thought I would, but it's lonely being a bachelor, I don't think I'm suited to it. It's been a long time. Perhaps you knew of my wife, did you?'

Carmichael shook her head and tactfully said nothing.

'I thought I'd never find anyone else whom I could love, a home-loving person, that means a lot, doesn't it? I'm sure you feel the same.' Nigel Denton went on in the same preoccupied way without waiting for an answer. Then he left the office after a friendly nod to Carmichael and proceeded through the department, glancing to each side as he went.

Carmichael was left sitting with the words running through her head: 'a home-loving person'. Was she a home-loving person? She had loved her cottage, loved doing the garden, loved having the cats, loved getting little suppers at night, but would she like doing it for two? Yes, yes, of course she would, it would be better than her present life. Not much, perhaps, with Derek Hanson, but better. To go to a consultant's cocktail party accompanied, not having to stand drink in hand waiting for somebody to speak to you. To go out to dinner together and to the theatre or cinema. Carmichael hated going to the theatre or to the movies because coming out of a crowded foyer full of chattering people and going by herself to her car made her feel especially lonely. Everyone seemed to be with someone else. Of course there must be other people who were alone like her, but she never seemed to see them and certainly wasn't conscious of them. After the theatre there seemed always to be a man calling for a taxi for his wife or girlfriend or saying, 'Wait here, I'll fetch the car' if it were raining. You stood there looking at the wet streets and waiting for a little pause in the downpour so that you could rush to your car. Yes, that was the lonely part. No status either. Not status exactly, but to belong, to be one of a pair – that was what she was fighting so hard to attain.

A staff nurse put her head round the door. 'There's an O.D. coming in, Sister. Shall I let that new nurse do the wash-out, while the doctor's there I mean, or would you rather . . .?'

Carmichael got up briskly. 'Yes, that would be a good idea. I haven't seen her do one and the doctors do prefer us to do them, don't they.' She smiled at the nurse absently and accompanied her to the nursing station.

'Do they know what she's taken?' she asked.

The nurse replied doubtfully: 'Well one of the ambulance men said he was bringing an empty bottle with Mogadon written on it. It was beside her so presumably it was that.'

'She'll probably be all right then,' said Carmichael, 'but we'd better get ready anyway.' The nurse nodded and left her. Carmichael stood by the nursing station tapping her fingers idly on the wooden surface.

At that moment Auxiliary Nurse Pearson, her face averted, walked by. Carmichael watched her figure, watched the twitching bottom that had diverted Derek Hanson's attention from herself. Yes, it was certainly going to be worth it. This nurse, Nurse Pearson, would probably get married and behave like a slut in the house if her nursing was anything to go by. She, Carmichael, would see to it that she was a good wife, she always did a job well, but the thought of bed – she still shied away from that. She was not sure of herself where any great intimacy was involved, not only with a man but with anyone else. She thought of last night's kiss and grimaced, not with pleasure but with a certain amount of distaste.

The ambulance men drew the trolley through to the theatre and Carmichael walked beside it, noting how deeply unconscious the woman was, and how loud her snores.

'Right, nurse, bring the wash-out trolley,' she said and the nervous staff nurse who had already prepared the stomach wash-out at the theatre table nodded as the patient was lifted from the ambulance trolley. The ambulance men drew out their poles from the canvas stretcher.

'How many is it this month, Sister? We've brought you three,' said one man and peered at the patient speculatively. Carmichael did not answer. The man made a rude sign to the staff nurse which Carmichael did not see.

'Ah, Dr Singh, we were waiting for you,' she said as Dr Singh walked into the theatre. 'May Nurse . . .?'

Dr Singh nodded his head and came up and raised the patient's eyelids. 'Mogadon, I hear,' he said.

Carmichael agreed and showed him the bottle that the ambulance man had brought into the theatre.

'Come along, nurse, introduce the tube,' said Carmichael, positioning the patient professionally. 'Is it properly lubricated?'

'Yes, Sister.' The staff nurse looked as if she would rather be anywhere but here at this moment, but she came forward holding the thick stomach tube between her finger and thumb and introduced it deftly and neatly through the patient's rather blue lips, to Carmichael's approval. The tube began to slide down. The patient coughed slightly and as she did so her body undulated on the table like a stranded fish. The tube was now well down the patient's gullet and a junior nurse raised the funnel attached now to the end of the tube and poured a small amount of the wash-out fluid into it. She looked questioningly at Carmichael who was standing beside the patient watching carefully.

'All right, nurse, you're safely in the stomach,' said Carmichael and some more water gurgled down the tube. The stomach wash-out proceeded, the funnel was turned upside down and the stomach contents began to run into the bucket, the acid smell making the junior nurse wrinkle her nose. The patient was an elderly woman, her white hair curled attractively round her head.

'Wonder what made her take an overdose, Sister,' said the staff nurse.

'Depression? That's the usual cause isn't it. Depression. Perhaps she'd lost her husband or something.' This was Dr Singh speaking. He stood close to the patient his hand on her pulse.

'The relatives will probably be able to tell us,' said Carmichael rather abruptly because she suddenly thought she had heard Derek Hanson's voice outside the theatre. She held herself firmly in check remembering how she had thought that people having an affair like Nigel Denton and Madeleine Taylor did not give proper attention to their work. She had rather altered her opinion now, she thought, and therefore would not let herself be seduced away from the operating table even if he was outside. It was surprising, she thought, how circumstances alter cases. She turned back to watch the stomach wash-out, the water was now running almost clear, the bucket beside the woman was half full and the patient was showing signs of coming round, moving her head restlessly to and fro, beginning to bite on the tube.

'Can you withdraw the tube now? I think that's enough,' said Dr Singh. The nurse looked at Carmichael and Carmichael nodded agreement.

13

Carmichael took some weeks to adjust to her new life, a life that was so altered, now that she was accompanied on her evenings out by Derek, and thought of him both on and off duty.

As the relationship appeared to Carmichael to grow deeper, she began to warm more and more to him and this warmth became almost an infatuation. She accepted his faults, or almost did so. She learned that he was arrogant in his opinions. He could be overbearing in manner in restaurants or clubs. Even when getting petrol at the garage he was apt to overdo the familiarity, the hail-fellow-well-met attitude. She knew these to be faults but she tried to overlook them. Also she learned that he had an eye for a pretty figure. Once she remarked on it. He smiled a rather secret debonair smile and defended himself.

'Well I've always liked women but you're the only one I'm interested in, you're such good company, so intelligent, so different from the others.' He had put out his hand and clasped her arm and drawn her close to him.

Carmichael tried to subdue her doubt and believe him, believe that he really did prefer her to the women he looked at. But although she was warming towards him, something made her draw back. She felt a natural fear of being let down, of losing him. She wasn't sure exactly on what she based this fear but as she grew accustomed to being kissed – although Derek was never particularly amorous: his love-making was mostly confined to fairly chaste kisses and holding hands – she felt somehow glad that she was not committing herself too quickly.

Carmichael wondered sometimes about this too. How would she handle a really passionate embrace? What would she do if he tried to become more intimate? So far, however, he had not, and as the relationship continued his behaviour remained the same.

They went out to dine – almost always to the same restaurant – they went to the movies, to a concert, for walks. Anything, any date was enough to make Carmichael feel that she was wanted and made her feel, too, that here was someone who thought of her, planned for her, as constantly as she thought of him when they were apart. She was entranced by the relationship – perhaps even more so when she was not with him.

One day when the sun had grown warmer, they took a picnic lunch to the river on Carmichael's day off. They sat on the bank talking comfortably together and eating Carmichael's excellent lunch. She had even bought a picnic basket with a Thermos flask and pretty plates, and she took tremendous pleasure in making sandwiches and salads for the two of them. Derek had brought along a bottle of wine. Carmichael sat there beside him on a rug that she had provided. The willows around them were rustling softly in the very slight warm breeze and the river in which he had cooled the wine drifted by slowly – romantically, Carmichael thought. She had read about such scenes in so many romantic novels. There was not a soul anywhere to be seen, the birds were singing – it was perfect, Carmichael thought. Just the place for him to propose to her and she suddenly wondered if he would. That was what she wanted more than anything, to be able to show a cluster of diamonds, a ring, on her left hand. She didn't mind how small the stones were as long as it was there, outward proof that she was no longer alone.

She glanced sideways at Derek. He was not looking at her, but was idly plucking pieces of grass and biting them and looking out over the water. There was silence for a long time and then he suddenly said something that made Carmichael feel almost faint, she was so certain he was going to propose marriage.

'I want to ask you something, Agnes, something I've been wanting to ask you for some time. I hope you won't think it too soon in our relationship for me to ask you such a thing. Please think carefully before you refuse.'

It was as much as Carmichael could do to still the trembling of her hands; she put them behind her, bracing herself, and glanced towards him, hoping she looked as attractive as possible. That was always her hope, she was still intensely careful of her make-up before she went out with Derek, but the sun, as she knew only too well, might do anything to it. She longed to take out her compact just to look and see if she was fit to receive a proposal of marriage, to see if she looked as good as it was possible for her to look, as much for Derek's sake as her own. She had a scarf round her head tied under the chin. Although this accentuated the sharpness of her nose it helped to hide her hair, which even in this slight breeze soon became ruffled and the fine baby-like texture was unruly, not pretty. But at least she felt confident about that. She turned to him.

'What, Derek, what do you want to ask me? she said, but she knew, she knew, she knew. It was, she thought, the most wonderful moment in a woman's life, to receive a proposal from a man she really wanted to make it. And could he have chosen a more perfect spot than here by the river? She thought not. He still did not look at her and she wondered why. Was he perhaps shy of asking this great question? Did he think she might say no? He must know she wouldn't refuse him. Surely the fact that she had been out with him so many times, had never repulsed any of his advances would have made him more confident. He wasn't young, but neither was she – still, he must be a good ten years older than herself, but that wouldn't deter him. He didn't speak, so Carmichael said again softly: 'What is it, Derek, please ask me, you know me well enough now.'

He still gazed at the river and began throwing little pieces of plucked grass away from him, and some flew across to Carmichael and she caught one of them in her hand and thought that that was in a way symbolic, that they were like little questions coming over from him to her and she knew what her answer would be. Of course he wanted to marry her and of course she would. His words interrupted her thoughts.

'I never like asking anyone for anything but I really am in rather a quandary.' He turned fully round and looked at her.

Carmichael sat upright, a vague feeling that this was not a proposal came over her. It didn't sound like one. She said nothing and Derek Hanson continued.

'I've got myself into a bit of a spot really. This dear old friend of mine, I think a lot of him, he's been badly let down by his business partner. They've only got a small business and he's come to me for help. Poor Tom, he's much too trusting. Anyway I promised to lend him two thousand pounds and now I find I can't raise it as easily as I thought. Could I possibly ask you . . .'

He put out his hand and covered hers, a gesture he often used. Before, it had always thrilled Carmichael but now she felt suspicion leap in her mind and then she was ashamed. After all, it was decent of him to lend money to a friend, to think about the friend, to care.

Her cottage had fetched over forty-five thousand pounds and even after paying off the mortgage there had been a sizeable sum left. When she wanted another house she would, of course, have to pay a lot more . . . Did this mean that Derek was asking to borrow money now and that the proposal might come next, not now perhaps, but later? Carmichael wanted time to think and said so.

'Of course I understand, of course I understand you must think about it, it's a lot of money, it's not something you can do just like that.' Derek's voice was low and understanding but he went on, 'You see, I'm saving too. I'm wanting to buy a house for . . .' His hand came over again and covered hers and squeezed it gently. 'Can't you guess?' he asked.

Carmichael knew that a more experienced woman would have pressed further but she could not, she dared not, she couldn't trust her voice.

'A house,' was all she said huskily.

'Of course, when I set up home with the woman I love I shall want to buy a house, that's why I don't want to sell my shares, at the moment I should have to sell at a loss and I must have a home to offer, mustn't I?' He gazed into her eyes longingly and lovingly and bent forward and touched his mouth to hers.

Carmichael felt reassured but couldn't quite understand what he meant, was this a proposal of marriage but in a roundabout way? Her shyness and nervousness again prevented her from taking the matter further but she decided there and then to let him have the two thousand.

The pressure of her lips must have told him so because he said, 'Dare I hope that you . . .?'   Carmichael thought for a moment that the proposal of marriage might come now, but no.

'Dare I hope that you will trust me, that you will lend me the money? It's only for a short time, I can raise it myself soon, but not in time for my friend. He may not want it for long, he's a good chap and he'll pay it back the moment he can.'

Carmichael put her hand up and gently touched Derek's lips. It was the first time she had ventured such a gesture.

'Please, please don't explain. Of course I trust you. If you want two thousand pounds to lend your friend I think it's very good of you and I will let you have it. I really can and I'll be pleased to.'

Hanson leant back on the sloping turf and let out a long sigh.

'Thank God you trust me. We must trust each other, Agnes, surely we must.'

'Of course I trust you, Derek.' Carmichael said it almost too hastily. 'Tomorrow I'll go to the building society.'

'Thank you.'

Derek's eyes were closed. He looked, Carmichael thought, suitably impressed by her generosity and at that moment she was happy and full of confidence that he was going to be her husband and that his money would be hers and hers his. It was a wonderful feeling. She was glad that she had acquiesced. How mean, how paltry if she hadn't. How could she think with one side of her mind that she wanted to marry him and with the other side that she couldn't trust him with two thousand pounds of her money. Indeed it would be a useless relationship if one thought like that.

The atmosphere between them as they finished their wine and then packed the basket was charged with feeling. Derek took every opportunity to touch her, stroke her arm and when at last they rose he put his arm round her waist and drew her to him. They kissed, his brown eyes gazed into hers – pools of sincerity, thought Carmichael, but smiled at herself, remembering what she had thought of his eyes when they first met.

'Why the smile?' asked Derek.

Carmichael shook her head, 'Nothing – your eyes reminded me of something I read a long time ago,' she said.

92

'I don't know how to thank you, Agnes,' he said as he picked up the picnic basket and the rug and they walked towards the car.

Carmichael gave a backward glance at the river, the willows and the lush grass and sighed a little, a sigh of regret that the afternoon was over. Still, this would cement their relationship even more firmly she told herself.

Next day Carmichael went to the building society the moment she was off duty and made arrangements to withdraw the money. It would take a few days, she was told. She felt a glow of satisfaction when she came out. She was meeting Derek tonight and she would be able to tell him what she had done. Her man, she thought to herself romantically. She gazed into the shops as she walked by on her way to the car-park, still filled with this glow of satisfaction and a new, even greater feeling of fondness for Derek. It meant a lot to Carmichael. She had hoarded her money carefully because before she met Derek it was all she had between herself and the rest of the world. She had always been careful, saving so that when she retired her pension would be sufficient and her home habitable and comfortable. This had always been so important, but now it had receded into a far distance, into almost nothing because her life was going to be shared.

No longer loneliness, no longer having to decide everything for herself, there'd be Derek beside her when they were married. Should she keep her car? Yes, she decided she must, she couldn't bear to get rid of her little Metro. Although she loved to sit beside Derek and be driven she still had an affection for her own vehicle. But perhaps Derek would say that one car was enough and let her drive his although he never had up to now, not that she had ever asked.

The thoughts were comforting and lovely and Carmichael wanted to prolong them, so on the way back to the car-park she went into a coffee house and sat there drinking coffee, still feeling the wonderful glow. She was someone, she was owned, she belonged. Now it was hardly necessary to say to Derek when they parted, 'When shall we meet again?' or 'When shall I see you again?' It was automatic. They saw each other at least three or four, sometimes more, times a week.

As she sipped her coffee Carmichael wondered idly what he did on the other nights. She never asked him and wouldn't dream of doing so, probably he did what she did, looked at television, went to bed early. She finished her coffee, paid for it and left the restaurant.

She needed stockings. In a department store she chose what she wanted and on her way out noticed a rack of men's ties. She picked a navy blue one with a small gold motif. Derek appeared to be rather conservative about his ties, and this looked the kind of tie he would choose. It was the first present she had ever bought him. It was neatly enclosed in a cellophane pack. She paid at the check-out and popped the tie into her handbag where it fitted easily without creasing. She then made her way towards the car-park.

Her car had become unbearably hot from standing in the sun and she sat in it for a moment with the window open waiting for the interior to cool a little. Suddenly, as she looked out through the windscreen at the blue sky above her and the mass of cars in front of her, a shaft of doubt went through her almost like a wound inflicted by a dagger. Was it right that he had asked her for money like this? Was he perhaps like all the others? Was he just after what he could get? No, no. She shook her head to and fro almost as if she was in pain and then saw herself doing so in the car mirror and stopped. Why was she suddenly feeling like this, what had made her begin to doubt? The fact that he had asked for money at all? Perhaps. But then why not, if they were so close and he was thinking of getting engaged? Probably when they were married they would have a joint account and trust each other completely. If they weren't prepared to do that how could they contemplate marriage? No, of course, it was all right.

Carmichael put the car into gear and gently moved backwards, forgetting that she had not put on her seat belt. She stopped the car with a jerk that was unlike her, belted up, backed the car a little further out and drove towards the hospital. Unhappily, it was a long time before the warm glow of satisfaction returned.

14

After her visit to the building society, Carmichael came on duty at two o'clock. She had spent a restful morning: she had got up late, done her washing and tidied her cupboards before going to town. Now she had recovered from the anxiety that she had experienced in the car and the warm, comfortable, satisfied feeling of something worth doing done had come back.

She approached the front of the hospital realizing she was a little early. She decided to spend some time in the changing room, maybe putting on a little more make-up since she had not repaired it before going out.

She walked through the swing doors into the spacious front hall of the hospital. Along one side were telephones and Carmichael looked idly towards them. The receptionist was absent from her usual place at the reception desk – she was probably still at lunch. Carmichael had paused by the desk when she noticed that her departmental nurse, Pearson, was making a telephone call. She stood there partically concealed by a plant listening to the girl's conversation, waiting for a chance to reprove her for being absent from the Casualty department and late on duty. The girl was still in mufti. The name she used in the first sentence made Carmichael stiffen.

'I've got to see you tonight, Derek,' the girl's voice was urgent and demanding. 'Well, it's true what I told you last night.' She paused, listening to the voice at the other end of the telephone, and then went on: 'Yes I have. Well, you said go and see and make sure and that's what I've done. We've got to talk about it.' Another pause, and then: 'Well, I can't help what you've told her, if the meeting takes longer than you think I'll wait, I'll be waiting. You know those shrubs at the back of the home? Well, I'll be there. You'll have to come without the car, just walk down and I'll wait for you. There's a seat there you know, we've been there before. You've just got to come, Derek, I've just got to talk it out with you.' The girl's voice rose. 'Well, I know, I know I'll need some money to get rid of it, but I haven't got any, you know that, you had my two hundred pounds.' The girl looked furtively round, but there was no one else in the front hall and Carmichael was hidden. 'That's what I want to talk to you about so don't forget to turn up or I'll come to the damn meeting.' The girl slammed down the phone and Carmichael melted away from the plant that concealed her and made her way to the changing room. She realized that Pearson would have to go to the changing room, too, so she went up the back stairs, not wanting to be seen by her.

A chaos of thoughts went through her mind. Was she talking to Derek, Derek Hanson, her Derek? She was almost certain she was. Derek had said he'd got a meeting that night and he was not coming for her at the nurses' home till 9.30. What had this girl done, what had she said about money? Carmichael could hardly think, she was shaking so.

When she got to the changing room she was followed in by Pearson. She felt she couldn't bear to face her so she shut herself in one of the lavatories and sat down on the seat trying to marshal her thoughts. What was it the woman had said? She tried to reconstruct the conversation. It sounded as if . . . Oh God, don't let it be true . . . It sounded as if she was telling him she was pregnant. 'Get rid of it', it must mean that, and money, what did she need money for but that? For a second she felt glad that she had not yet given Derek the money. But what did that matter, what did that matter against losing him? She must be sure, absolutely sure that what she suspected was right. She rubbed her face with her hand careless of her make-up. She would be there somewhere tonight, perhaps hide in the shrubs. She knew exactly where the girl meant. She knew the place, at the back of the home there was a hard teak bench that no one ever used. She'd never seen anyone using it, it was surrounded by rhododendrons, almost hidden. The bushes must have been there before the home was built for they were well established, big plants. She'd sat there once or twice herself, reading. It was secluded and was the only place in the grounds where there was any shade from the sun. She'd have to get off early tonight. She wouldn't change when she came off duty, she'd be there in the shubbery waiting for them, listening to everything they said to each other – if it was Derek, her Derek.

A terrible flood of jealousy and disappointment came over her. She felt lonely again and then reached a sudden resolution. She thought: I could get rid of the girl, I've got rid of people before. Why should I let this girl snatch from me what I want? She wasn't going to give up easily; this was her chance to lose her loneliness for the rest of her life, and she wouldn't allow this woman to interfere.

By the time Carmichael came out of the lavatory, Debbie Pearson had gone. She got into her uniform mechanically, and as she looked in the big mirror she caught sight of her ashen face. She put her handbag down on the table and got out her make-up. She applied a little rouge quite expertly to both cheeks. She had to look completely normal. She went out of the room and downstairs. Her knees felt like jelly and she feared she was about to collapse but, gradually, as she walked towards the Casualty department, her resolution helped her. Nothing, nothing should take Derek away from her. She no longer doubted that it was he to whom Debbie Pearson had been talking. True, there could be other Dereks, but the meeting? He had told her he would be late, that he would come round to the home as soon as the meeting ended. There was no question of doubt.

She walked firmly into her department, gazing round to see if she could see the nurse whom she would have to destroy. She couldn't. Pearson was obviously already in one of the cubicles helping with a dressing. She would be no great loss, no loss at all to the department. Carmichael remembered her neglect of the old lady who had fallen out of the chair and her roughness towards children. It would be quite easy. She would find a way. The method would fall into her lap as it always did. She greeted her junior sister who smiled at her, not so much out of love for her, Carmichael thought bitterly, but because when Carmichael walked into the department at two o'clock she was able to leave.

97

'I'm sorry I'm late, Madeleine,' she said and they both walked towards her office. Sister Taylor gave her a brief report on what had happened during the morning, the disposal of the patients, who had had to be admitted and who had been discharged back to their own doctors. Carmichael listened and took it in with one part of her mind, reading the report as she did so.

'I'm off then, Sister Carmichael. Are you all right? You are a bit pale.'

Carmichael was aware that Madeleine Taylor gave her a curious look but she nodded her head vaguely and watched her junior sister walk out of the department. She noticed her slim, attractive figure, the way her long hair moved slightly as she walked. She was always neat, always trim thought Carmichael, and always attractive to men. She shook that thought off, she had her own man to cope with and she couldn't think of other people.

At the door of Casualty Nigel Denton appeared as if to meet Madeleine Taylor. The two walked off together and Carmichael noticed that they linked hands. The action disturbed Carmichael. She tried to dismiss it and turned again to the report book, read it briefly and then walked out and started to inspect the casualties who were in at the moment.

She had to get through the afternoon and evening, she had to make it pass, then she would be there, there where Derek and this beastly nurse were meeting. No doubt she'd entrapped him, Pearson was that kind of woman, thought Carmichael.

The nurses in the department that afternoon noticed no change in their sister. Carmichael was sure of that. She kept herself rigidly at her work, banishing from her mind the thought of the night.

A screaming child with a cut foot was dealt with expertly by the Casualty officer. Another small child who'd crushed his fingers in the door of a washing machine was also attented to and an elderly woman had to have stitches in her forearm which she had cut quite badly trying to open a tin of corned beef.

The inevitable trivial casualties flowed through the department as they always did, and then, late in the evening, after Carmichael had been to her supper, car crash victims were admitted: three people seriously hurt and a fourth with cuts and bruises. Carmichael wondered how it could be that in a car containing four people three could be so badly injured and the fourth only superficially. One day she would write an article on this kind of thing for the *Nursing Mirror*, she thought, and it pleased her that she was now so under control that she could think this way.

She dealt with the injured with the aid of the doctors and waited on Nigel Denton's registrar who was called down to see the patients with bad fractures. It was all routine, all slightly unreal.

When the time came to go off duty and the patients had been admitted leaving the department momentarily clear, Carmichael sighed a long sigh of relief. She went into her office and picked up her cloak and wrapped it round her. Even as she was walking out of Casualty she knew that this wearing of a cloak in summer amused her nurses, for it was a warm sultry evening. One or two people had remarked on the humidity and said that there was going to be a storm. She made sure that the cloak completely covered her uniform. This evening she was wearing it for another purpose. She bade goodnight to her nurses who replied politely, she also greeted the on-coming night staff. She was not usually so punctual and she had left her staff nurse to give the report to the night Casualty sister.

She hurried to the front door of the hospital. Out of the corner of her eye she saw Auxiliary Nurse Pearson making her way to the changing room. That was good, it would give her plenty of time to get settled in her hiding place. It was strange how Pearson had now become a person rather than a nurse, a person to be reckoned with, a rival. She watched her go up the stairs.

Carmichael walked swiftly. It was quite a little way but she didn't want to walk too quickly in case it attracted anyone's attention. The few people she met gave her no greeting, she didn't know any of them.

As she approached the home, she skirted the front door, went past a row of windows and round to the back. She was glad of the thickness of the clump of rhododendrons, the other trees were still too young to hide anybody. She made her way to where the couple had agreed to meet. The seat among the

99

shrubs looked new, the couple of times she had sat there she had found the varnish or creosote still slightly sticky. Now she moved further back from the seat to where the bushes were taller and where she could stand comfortably. She took off her paper cap, it would gleam too white. The evening was beginning to be dark and overcast. She crushed the hat up and slipped it into her pocket and wrapped her cloak more firmly round her. She stood and prepared herself to wait.

It was not long before she heard in the stillness the patter of feet on the tarmac leading down to the home, but it was not the nurse for whom she was waiting, but two or three other nurses returning to the nurses' home laughing and talking. This happened once or twice more, inevitably since they were all coming off duty. Carmichael waited, hearing the doors swing to behind them. Suddenly the clasp of her handbag, which she was holding tightly, snapped open and in the dim light she could see her building society passbook. She put her hand to the bag, intending to shut it but, missing the clasp in the gathering gloom, encountered the cellophane-wrapped tie which she had intended to give Derek this evening. She smiled a little. Well, she would give it to him she supposed, but first she would listen to what he had to say to Nurse Pearson.

She stood perfectly still as Nurse Pearson walked across to the seat and sat down. She had changed and was in a flowered frock with a light coat over it. She sat there, her foot swinging to and fro impatiently, and Carmichael, peering through the gloomy shrubbery, was, for some reason, amused. Any moment now he would come. Almost before she had time to think any more she heard his voice.

'God, you've chosen a dark enough spot.'

'Oh, you've got here then.' Pearson's voice was petulant.

'Well, the meeting wasn't too bad, they yacked on, of course, as usual, but I got out. Now what is it you want to talk about? You know what you've got to do, for goodness' sake. You know what you've got to do, don't you?' He sat down on the seat beside the woman and lit a cigarette. This surprised Carmichael. She had never seen Derek smoke before. Pearson flinched – she seemed more cross than tragic – and Carmichael listened, leaning forward a little so as to catch every word.

15

Carmichael had trembled slightly at the first sound of Derek's voice. She was afraid, too, that he might see her or sense she was there. But there was really no cause for alarm. The rhododendrons had been there long before the nurses' home was built. They were tangled and thick and had been left because of their attractiveness in the early summer when they bloomed prolifically. They concealed her well. It was becoming more and more overcast and the evening itself was getting darker. There was a moon, but it was obliterated every few seconds by scudding clouds, and across to the east Carmichael saw thicker, heavier clouds looming up towards them, slightly tinged with the orangey glow that marks a storm.

'If I had it done I should need at least a hundred pounds of my money back from you, perhaps more, you don't get this kind of thing done for nothing you know.' Pearson's voice was soft but shrewish.

'I know that, but I haven't got the money to hand. I wanted it, as I told you, to lend to a friend and I've done that, so I don't know what I'm going to do or what you're going to do.'

'Oh, I bet you lent it to a friend,' Debbie Pearson's voice became a little louder as she indicated her disgust. 'Put it on a horse more likely, knowing you, or spent it on some other woman. Don't think it's as easy to take me in as it is your darling Agnes Carmichael.'

Carmichael had difficulty in suppressing a gasp of anger and pain, but her rage was all directed against the woman. Pearson would bring out the worst in any man. However, she still had that little nagging feeling of relief that she hadn't yet given him anything, and that her money was still safe. She drew slightly nearer so as not to miss a word.

'No, but you're a damn sight more easily laid. She's a decent woman, Agnes. You wouldn't begin to understand her. I respect her.'

'Respect her my fanny!' I bet you're trying to get money out of her too, she's not your type and you know it, she's much too stiff and prissy, she's a real old maid.'

Carmichael stood tense and still, so tense that her limbs were beginning to ache. She tried to relax and looked up for a moment at the darkened sky. A distant rumble of thunder broke the momentary silence, then Derek spoke again. In the interval of silence Carmichael had heard a match strike and realized that one of them had lit a cigarette. She saw the brief glow but nothing more. When Derek spoke she realized that he had risen to his feet.

'How would you know what my type is?' His voice grated with anger.

Debbie Pearson interrupted him: 'I don't want to get rid of this child, anyway, I don't want to get rid of it and I'm not going to.' She raised her voice and Derek raised his in answer. Up until now they had been talking fairly quietly.

'Don't want to get rid of it, you bloody little fool. Why you ever got it in the first place I can't think. You're a nurse and you should know better, what with the pill and every other contraceptive device.' Their voices were so loud that Carmichael wondered if anyone else would hear them and she shrank back a little.

'Shut up. Do you want the whole home to hear us? It's marriage I want if you must know. I'm thirty-three and it may be my last chance to have a kid and while you're not exactly the man I'd choose, well you'll do, you'll have to.'

Lights were beginning to spring up in the nurses' home windows one after the other as more nurses came off duty. Carmichael drew further back into the shadows. One window, curtained but still showing light through, illuminated eerily the two people so near her.

'Marriage! Christ almighty! I wouldn't marry you if you were the last woman living. Anyway, how can I be sure it's my kid? Everybody knows your reputation for bed-hopping.'

'You bastard, Derek. I will have it and it is yours. You'll bloody well marry me or I'll spill the beans about it all to your bloody Carmichael, tell her what a randy bugger you are. I don't know how you've kept your hands off her all this time, even if she is an old bitch, an old calcified virgin.'

'Do what the hell you like. I'm through with arguing with you,' Hanson said, 'and if you say a word to Agnes Carmichael I'll cut your bloody throat.' He turned away and, in the dim light of the now curtained windows, Carmichael saw him start to walk away. She was shocked. She could not believe that he had spoken like that, she had never heard him speak roughly.

Debbie Pearson, still seated, put out a hand to stop him but he shook her off. It was clear that she was beginning to regret what she had said. She started to cry and put her other hand out and caught his and he shook that off as well and strode away. She sat there huddled on the seat; whether her crying was real or not Carmichael couldn't tell, nor did she care. This terrible woman's very presence seemed to have turned her Derek from the gentle, polite man Carmichael knew to one she did not recognize.

She moved gingerly forward, treading carefully – her actions now were almost mechanical. This promiscuous, pregnant, common woman must not be allowed to upset her Derek, not be allowed to upset their future together. She, Pearson, was nothing, just an incident in their lives, an unfortunate incident, yes, but men were like that. No doubt there had been many more women in Derek's life, but once she was married to him that would all stop. He had said he respected her, that was a start, and it gave her a warm feeling . . . Respect was a good start, passion Carmichael did not anticipate, nor perhaps love as other couples knew it, but to own him, to know he was hers, to know she was his, that was what she wanted. That kind of relationship was based on respect. Perhaps later they would grow closer together. Meanwhile nothing must be allowed to stand in the way.

These thoughts rushed through Carmichael's mind as she drew near the girl seated on the teak seat. She was really crying and had covered her face with her hands.

Carmichael felt no pity. She looked down at her handbag,

gently withdrew the tie intended as a present for Derek and moved forward with a stiff movement like an automaton. The cellophane packet covering the tie rustled slightly and fell at her feet. Debbie Pearson had taken a tissue out of her handbag and was wiping her eyes. The white of the paper handkerchief showed up in the dark. Suddenly a flash of lightning revealed the woman plainly and Carmichael could see the tears running down her made-up face smudging her mascara, then darkness again. Debbie Pearson half turned, the sky was again bright with another flash of sheet lightning. Carmichael's cloak had fallen to the ground. The last thing Debbie Pearson must have seen was the dark strip of material between Carmichael's hands and almost the last thing she must have felt was it tightening round her neck. She clawed at her throat and at Carmichael's hands but it was no use, it was too late.

Carmichael felt the strength pour into her. The woman below her on the bench was strong but not as strong as she, not in this moment. As the woman struggled she tightened the tie more firmly and tied first one knot, then a second, then, driven by an old memory, she hardly knew from where, she withdrew her nurses' scissors from her pocket, inserted them in the knot at the side of Pearson's neck and started to twist the scissors, twist and twist. Tighter and tighter grew the tie until suddenly Pearson slumped on to the seat, quiet and still. Her tongue was showing slightly between her lips, her eyes were open and protruded more prominently than they had in life. Carmichael looked at her and knew she was dead. She withdrew her scissors, put them back in her pocket and looked without emotion at the crumpled figure which had fallen slightly forward and was half off, half on the seat. She bent down to reassure herself that she had done the task she had set herself perfectly, that there was no life left. A flash of forked lightning lit up the blue face and Carmichael was satisfied. Something gleamed at her feet in the flash of lightning, it was the cellophane packet that had contained the tie, the present for Derek. Well, she could get him another. Now the tie was just a thin strip of material embedded in the fleshy neck of the woman in front of her.

Carmichael drew back, looked up and checked the windows

of the nurses' home. No one could possibly have seen her and there had been hardly any sound. Some of the curtains were drawn, others not, but even so no direct light reached the spot where she stood. Anyway, Carmichael knew no one would be looking, she was never so unlucky as to be spied upon.

Unhurriedly she picked up the cellophane packet, put it in her handbag and snapped the bag shut. As she did so large spots of rain struck the grass round her and the thunder grew louder. She picked up her cloak, flung it round her shoulders and walked round to the side of the home. As she was about to make her way to the doors two nurses emerged, laughing. In the darkness she watched them cross the drive quickly because of the rain, get into a small car, still chattering, still laughing, and drive away. Only then did she come out of the shadows and go into the home and to her room, meeting no one.

Inside she changed her uniform for an attractive summer dress. Her hands felt scored and she looked at them to find they were red with the stretching of the material of the tie, red with twisting the scissors. She soaked them in cold water and then dried them carefully on a towel, inspecting her nails as she did so, putting on hand lotion. Then she repaired her make-up quickly and skilfully and when at last Derek Hanson's familiar knock came on her door called, 'Come in, darling.'

Derek found her standing in the middle of her little sitting room smiling, waiting for him. It was the first time Carmichael had used the word 'darling' to Derek Hanson and she saw the quick look of surprise on his face as the door opened. She felt at ease and curiously exhilarated. And yet perhaps it was not curious, she had always felt like that when . . . The act she had just performed in the garden was almost banished from her mind and yet she knew it was the cause of her feeling of well-being. She had rid her life, their lives, of someone who might have jeopardized their future. However committed Derek had been, he was now free again. His kiss she received as usual without passion, but she received it with more welcoming warmth, more response that she had done before. She smelled brandy on Derek's breath but made no comment.

'Your meeting went on for a long time just as you predicted it would,' she said, almost gaily. 'What do you men find to talk about? I am sure you take a great deal longer than women would.' She was quite light-hearted, laughing, different. Derek Hanson looked at her curiously and then at his watch.

'Quarter to ten. As late as that,' he said. 'I'm sorry, Agnes, but never mind. We've just got time to go to Hatchers End for a drink.'

Carmichael agreed and handed him her coat to hold out for her. As she slipped into it she was conscious of a quick caress on her arms. She did not respond.

They walked out to his car in silence, but it was a companionable silence and she felt wonderful as he opened the car door and shut it carefully after her, running quickly round the car because now the rain was pouring down and the lightning and thunder came more frequently. She was not afraid of the storm; some times storms made her feel unsettled, nervous, but not now, not with Derek by her side. She felt somehow that she would never feel afraid of storms again, and that they would have a pleasant memory for her.

In familiar Hatchers End they sat comfortably. Carmichael felt the place suited her mood.

'I think I'll get myself a double brandy, that meeting took it out of me,' said Derek.

'I'll have a brandy too,' said Carmichael.

'You will?' Derek sounded surprised.

Carmichael smiled. 'Yes, I've had rather a hard day too,' she said.

Derek hesitated and looked as if he were about to say something, but evidently thought better of it and made for the bar.

Carmichael watched him fondly. He looked pale and strained, older than usual, ill at ease.

That meeting did take it out of you, Derek – it certainly did. But it was the second meeting, not the first, I fancy that did the worst damage to you, she thought to herself, but you needn't worry about it, my darling. I'll solve your problems, I'll solve all your problems if necessary, just as long as you are my . . . She watched him carefully carrying the two glasses across to the table. He put one in front of her and a small bottle of ginger ale on the table between them. She smiled at him: a reassuring,

106

comforting smile.

'I only got you a single but you can have a double if you wish. Thought you wouldn't be used to it – I haven't seen you drink very much, ever. Not spirits at any rate, except a liqueur. Is that all right, a single I mean?'

She looked at him again, still smiling. 'Yes, yes, that's fine, Derek,' she said. 'Everything's all right,' she added, though of course at that moment he would not understand what she meant.

After another leisurely drink they drove back to the nurses' home. The storm had abated somewhat and now the flashes of sheet lightning and the distant rumbling of thunder were further away. Carmichael hoped that after the conversation she had heard between Derek and Nurse Pearson he would not refer again to the money he wanted to borrow, not this evening anyway. She was conscious that the passbook was still in her handbag and also that she had forgotten to get rid of the empty cellophane packet. She must get him another tie tomorrow. In her off duty she would make a special journey. Perhaps she would get something a little different, she didn't fancy that kind of tie now, not after . . . It would be nice to introduce him to a slightly more colourful tie, something more . . . well, she would choose it, it would be to her taste and she would see if he liked it.

The rain was still falling in large thundery drops as they stopped outside the nurses' home. Derek Hanson switched off the engine and the headlights and they sat there together. It was usual for him now to put his arm round her shoulders, draw her to him and kiss her gently. This she liked, but she was still not sure yet how she would cope with any more intimate caresses. He didn't try, he leaned back in his seat again and looked at her almost absent-mindedly and then said: 'I like that place – Hatchers End – do you?'

'Yes, I do. It's comfortable and quiet and very well appointed, yes, I like it.'

'We'll have dinner there one night and see what it's like. We haven't dined there and I've heard the food is very good.'

Carmichael nodded her head in agreement, watching him closely. He still looked, she thought, rather ill, rather pale.

'Did you see what I saw behind the potted palm?' he asked suddenly, amusement tingeing his voice.

Carmichael looked at him quickly. 'No, what do you mean, Derek?' she asked.

'Oh, of course your back was to them. It was our Mr Nigel Denton and your Sister Taylor, sitting very close together. I don't know whether they'd had dinner there, they were just having drinks when I saw them. I didn't know they were going out together, I didn't know they were sweet on each other.'

'I did. Yes, Madeleine Taylor told me all about it.' The words 'sweet on each other' no longer upset Carmichael, no longer made her feel jealous. She remembered how she had seen Nigel Denton and Madeleine Taylor link fingers as they had walked away from her department. It was so nice to feel comfortable about such a thing, not to feel a wild intolerable jealousy.

'Yes, they're very well suited to each other. He's such a nice man and Madeleine Taylor, well, she's most attractive I think,' she said warmly.

'You knew him in another hospital, didn't you? I believe you told me that.'

Carmichael nodded absently. 'I did.' She realized how the change in her life had made so much difference to her. She no longer wondered about Nigel Denton, about his drinking, no longer surmised how he felt about his wife's death, no longer wondered if he had had affairs since then. Indeed, she was hardly interested in him at all except, of course, as a consultant in charge of her department. She realized as she sat there that other people's lives were not interesting to her now because she had a life of her own and it was so full.

She turned suddenly to Derek and put her hand over his. It was one of the very few times she had made such a gesture. He took her hand and squeezed it between both of his.

'You're a very nice person, Agnes, a very nice person,' he said with such genuine feeling that Carmichael reacted to it with all her heart. She knew only too well it was not love she felt for this man and probably not love he felt for her, but it was something perhaps even better than love. She would protect him always, he would need it. He had failings, weaknesses. She was not sure that he would protect her, she was not sure even

108

that he would be faithful to her, but that didn't matter, she wanted him and she believed he knew it.

After a while he got out of the car and came round and opened the door for her, and escorted her up the steps to the door of the home and held it open for her.

'Good night, Agnes,' he said and leaned forward, his lips touching her cheek. Then he turned and started to make his way back to his car.

She was almost disappointed because she had suddenly felt she would like to ask him in for a cup of coffee, although she was nervous, fearful of having him in her room. But she stood there, just inside the glass doors, and watched the red tail-lights disappear up the drive. It was only when they were completely out of sight that she gave a thought to the body which must still be there, half on and half off the seat. By now it must be saturated. The thought made her smile to herself.

She went to her room and locked the door behind her, crossed over to the window to check that it too was locked. She stood there looking out, but could see only the dull outline of the shrubs. She thought for a moment that the flasher wouldn't be out on a night like this, that was rather a pity. He would have had a nasty surprise waiting for him if he'd gone in to those shrubs. Well, perhaps the rain hadn't put him off. She got ready for bed and once there immediately fell asleep.

Something woke her in the middle of the night. She sat up in bed suddenly terrified. Something had bumped against her window. Or had she dreamed it? She couldn't be sure. Trembling, she got out of bed, crossed the room and parted the curtains gently. She peered out. It was dark and the rain appeared to have stopped but there were still clouds obliterating the moon. She could see little of the view in front of her through the glass, just the slight gleam of the wet path. She had not put on her light. For some reason she dared not. She could feel her heart thudding violently. For a moment she had thought – yes, she admitted it to herself that Nurse Pearson had got up and was trying to get into the nurses' home by banging on the glass of her window. That was ridiculous.

Carmichael drew the curtains again almost violently and sat down on the side of her bed. Then she lay down, still listening. It must have been something in a dream or perhaps something had blown against her window. But she didn't remember what she had been dreaming. For the rest of the night she lay awake, trying hard to concentrate on the time spent with Derek that evening, the various inflections of his voice, the expressions that had crossed his face and the nice sweet taste of the brandy, but she found it hard to shut out another face, make-up smudged, wet with tears, bloated and blue, lips parted, the tongue just visible.

At last she could stand it no longer. She got up and walked to and fro across her room, quietly, taking small paces, to the window, to the door; to the window, to the door, quietly on bare feet. She went through into her other room and back again. She felt contempt for herself for not being able to control her own thoughts. Surely she was able to do that now? She didn't want to become obsessive – that was the word, she thought, obsessive about getting rid of someone who so badly needed dismissal, not only from her department but from the world itself.

She had done it and she had done it before. Now this was just someone else added to the number, someone who needed to be despatched, someone who could not be trusted to treat other people properly. Her heart slowed down a little and she began to feel better. She bathed her face in cold water, then got back into bed – she felt cold – but when morning came she was still awake, still staring fixedly at the drawn curtains of her bedroom.

16

The next morning Carmichael walked up the drive from the nurses' home to go on duty. She walked more slowly than usual, for she was already in uniform, not having gone to the changing room the previous evening, and therefore could go straight to the Casualty department. She did not encourage her nurses to wear their uniforms home but last night, she thought with a slight grimace, had been an exception.

The sunlight glistened on drops of water on the blades of grass. Each side of the tarmac the sun shone on the pools from last night's rain and Carmichael wondered fleetingly how Pearson, or what was left of her, had fared in the storm.

The wet earth smelled pleasant and she felt elated, fulfilled, at one with other people. She felt an understanding of their problems. This, she thought, was because of her changed prospects and her ability – no, her genius – of being able to deal with Derek's problems as easily as she had always managed her own.

As she walked along, thoughts of marriage were uppermost in her mind. She was rather surprised that this was so after having heard the conversation between her husband-to-be and his . . . she hesitated before using the word – his paramour. She also thought of the form she had filled in to allow her to withdraw two thousand pounds from the building society to give to Derek. Last night had not changed that. She felt that was the kind of man he was and she must put up with it. She felt indulgent towards him, she would change him, or at least curtail some of his extravagances, if necessary his affairs. In the romantic novels she had read there had always been a difficult man. Sometimes he had been brutal and taciturn, but the heroine – and she placed herself in that rôle – had always managed to tame him, to make him gentle, easy to live with. Perhaps Derek would never be entirely like that but he would be hers as far as the wedding ring was concerned, and hers too, probably, as far as money was concerned. For the rest, well she would just have to watch him, look after him, see that he never again got into the clutches of a woman like the one she had disposed of.

Half-way up the long drive Carmichael met Tony, one of the young gardeners. She liked him, for he talked to her and occasionally gave her a bunch of flowers from the garden for her sitting room – strictly against the hospital rules. He was wheeling a bicycle and pointed with a half smile to the front wheel, the tyre of which was punctured.

'Having to walk this morning, Sister,' he said and for a moment stopped, leaning on his bicycle, the handlebars of which caught the sunshine and speared the light.

'What a nuisance for you, when did you do that?' asked Carmichael with more than her usual friendliness and animation.

He grinned back at her. 'Last night. Had to walk all the way here this morning, but I'll mend it in the firm's time.' He flung the remark back at her as he proceeded, pointing again at the tyre and laughing. Carmichael tried to look reproving but failed and they parted amicably.

She looked up and down the road as she came to the junction of the drive, crossed and made her way to the hospital. She looked again to see if the senior gardener or any other of the junior boys were around, but no one else was in sight. She was rather sorry, she would have preferred someone else to have found . . . Still, it could not be helped. She gave an imperceptible shrug of her shoulders and straightened her back.

She walked to the hospital, her cloak blowing round her. She wondered again as she walked if she would give up her job when she married. It didn't really matter. She would be Sister Hanson, of course. She thought of Jones. What a thing to be able to tell her. Well, when she came on that visit maybe there would be an engagement ring to show her. That would be something to impress Jones, decidedly more important than being made a nursing officer.

She made her way through the front door of the hospital and gave an almost cheery greeting to a surprised telephonist whom she usually ignored or at the most nodded curtly to.

In the department she was greeted almost at once by her junior staff nurse, Nurse Burton, who came towards her, head on one side, hands raised in mock resignation.

'No Nurse Pearson again, Sister Carmichael,' she said. 'I wonder what's the matter this time? Probably she's got her period, or her mother's ill, or her grandmother's died.'

Carmichael did not feel altogether happy with this remark and almost snapped at the nurse, her good humour vanishing.

'Well, it may be something genuine this time. The trouble is she's cried wolf so many times that we're apt not to believe her.'

'I suppose so, but I hope we get someone. It's the finger clinic this morning,' said the staff nurse, making her way past her senior sister.

Carmichael went into her office and dialled the nursing officer to tell her of Nurse Pearson's absence. Strangely she did this without even a thought of the girl she had seen last night, slumped half on, half off the seat in the shrubbery whom the gardener might well have found by now. No, it was just as if a nurse was missing from the department, a nurse short in the finger clinic, someone ill or detained in some way. It was as if Pearson really was off sick, was playing truant or skiving as she very often did. There was an exasperated sigh at the other end of the phone as the nursing officer answered.

'OK, Carmichael. Finger clinic, isn't it? I'll try and send you someone, but goodness knows where I'm going to get anyone, we're short everywhere.'

'Thanks. As quick as you can, if you will, patients start coming early you know.' Carmichael put the phone down and divested herself of her cloak, went to the window and looked out. It was only then that the reality of the absence of Nurse Pearson struck her, she realized why she was not there. This window did not look in the direction of the nurses' home but on the back of the hospital with its well-kept lawns and flower beds, small trees, and young saplings. As yet no vandals had done anything to the hospital grounds but this caused more surprise than complacency.

As Carmichael looked out she saw two of the gardeners walking across the lawn talking, one wheeling a barrow. Well, they certainly weren't with Tony, she thought. She was bothered by the thought that that boy would find Nurse Pearson, but still, she'd already thought about that and it couldn't be helped.

She wondered where Derek was this morning, whether she'd see him. She thought of last night, of their intimacy and then remembered how he'd told her about Taylor and Nigel Denton and the pleasure that she had taken in the knowledge that they had been at Hatchers End together. She thought of the difference in her own feelings. It was wonderful being cushioned against bitterness and jealousy. She went out into the Casualty department and began her day's work with enthusiasm and zest. She spoke to the nurses with less of her usual tartness.

It was not until nearly eleven o'clock that the news Carmichael was expecting seeped through to Casualty. A white-faced junior, fresh from her morning coffee break, came up to her, banging on her office door with unnecessary force.

'What is it, nurse?' Carmichael asked, but when she saw the girl's face she knew only too well what it was.

'It's Pearson, Sister, Nurse Pearson, she's been found, near the nurses' home. Tony, the gardener, found her. He's outside in the Casualty waiting room. He says he was sent to the canteen for a coffee. He's in a terrible state. Do you want to see him?'

'Why, what's happened' asked Carmichael inwardly congratulating herself on her completely innocent expression and blank face.

'She's been killed by that man, that Peeping Tom, the flasher. She's been strangled, that's what he says. She was all wet and . . . She's in the mortuary.' The girl suddenly burst into tears.

'My goodness, how terrible!' Carmichael felt she showed just the right amount of astonishment and horror. 'Now take it steadily, nurse. Come in here and sit down for a moment.' Carmichael placed the nurse in the chair opposite hers. 'Now just sit there quietly for a moment. Here, take this.' She handed

114

the girl a tissue from a box on the desk. 'I'll go and see Tony.'
She walked through the department steadily. One or two of the
nurses looked curiously at her, they'd seen the young nurse's
white face.

Carmichael went out into the waiting room and there was
Tony, shaking like a leaf, his usual ruddy complexion as pale as
that of the nurse in Carmichael's office. There was no one else
in the waiting room, all the patients were inside getting ready to
have their fingers looked at by Dr Singh.

Carmichael sat down beside the young boy. She was going to
ask him what she really wanted to know – what Pearson had
looked like after being out all night in the storm. She was
certain now that Pearson was dead. Of course, last night she
had been certain but that bump on her window had frightened
her.

'Now, tell me exactly what happened, Tony, tell me slowly
please.' She placed a reassuring hand on his arm, an unusual
gesture.

'I mended the puncture after I'd seen you, Sister Carmichael,
because Mr Malcolm, the head gardener, he was in the hospital
grounds and I thought I'd better do it while he was away.'

Carmichael nodded, curbing her impatience.

'Then I got out the edgers, that's what he said I was to do,
edge the lawn because it was too wet to mow, and I started.
Then when I got near those shrubs – you know where the seat
is?' He looked at her his eyes wide and red-rimmed and
Carmichael nodded. 'Well, I saw something there and first of all
I thought it was a bag of laundry, I did straight, a bag of
laundry. I went to look and I saw her face. It was terrible, it was
blue, blue and sort of white, mottled and there was something
round her neck I don't know what it was, but I could see she
was dead. I've never seen anyone dead before but I knew she
was dead. It's that man, Sister, the flasher, he strangled her.'

He buried his face in his hands and Carmichael pressed his
arm again. He continued. 'Mr Malcolm came, thank God, and
he rang the police and they came, panda cars and everything,
and they took photos and asked me questions. I seemed to be
there for ages. The ambulance came . . . and then they sent me
off to the canteen to get some coffee, but I felt so sick. I went to

115

the canteen and tried to drink it but I couldn't, they gave it to me free but I couldn't drink it so I came in here. I saw the ambulance take her to the mortuary. It was awful, Sister Carmichael.'

Carmichael stood up. 'Come with me,' she said. She led him out of the Casualty waiting room and up the stairs towards Miss Thompson's office. She knocked.

'Come in, who is it?' Miss Thompson's voice was as usual crisp and business-like.

'Wait there just a minute, Tony.' Carmichael went in and closed the door behind her. Miss Thompson looked up.

'What is it, Agnes? I've sent you the replacement.'

'There's been a nurse found strangled outside the nurses' home. It's Auxiliary Nurse Pearson. She was found in the garden. I've got the garden boy here outside, he found her and I don't quite know what to do with him, he's in a bit of a state. They sent him to the canteen to get some coffee and he felt sick so he came to Casualty.'

Thompson stood up. She looked incredulous. 'Strangled? Pearson? Dead you mean?'

An inane remark, thought Carmichael, but kept her face suitably composed.

'Yes, indeed. According to Tony she's in the mortuary at the moment. It's really been a terrible shock to the boy and I felt I must ask your advice as to what to do with him. I'm sure there will be a lot more questioning. I suppose he came into Casualty because he didn't know where else to go. I suppose really he comes under Casualty's auspices in a way.'

Thompson looked more angry than shocked.

'What was she doing there? That terrible man, that Peeping Tom, why haven't they caught him?'

'I don't know,' said Carmichael. 'At the moment I don't know any more than you do. Tony just found her there and it was a great shock to him. He's never seen anyone dead before.'

The nurse in Thompson came uppermost. 'Bring him in. I'll cope with the poor kid,' she said. Carmichael opened the door and motioned Tony in. He went in shakily and Thompson put a chair for him to sit down on opposite her. Carmichael made for the door of Thompson's office.

'I must get back to my department, we're very busy and that girl you sent me isn't . . .'

'She was the best I could do, Agnes, and of course, yes, get back and thank you.' Thompson sounded rather off balance.

As she was about to shut the door Carmichael said, 'Shall I have some coffee sent up for you, or something?'

Thompson nodded as Carmichael withdrew and made her way back to the Casualty department.

Things had worked out rather as she had thought. She was sorry it had to be Tony to see such a sight, the boy wasn't used to that kind of thing, but who was? Perhaps it would have been better if a nurse had found the body, but then on the other hand a nurse wouldn't go round to the back of the home usually, not first thing in the morning, only a gardener would.

In a way she was glad that Pearson had been found. She wondered what she looked like, whether they had taken the tie off her neck, it must have been drenched and the knot difficult to undo. Tony's description of her was anything but enlightening. Well, that woman Pearson would not fool about with her, Carmichael's, fiancé again, nor would she be around to be nasty to patients or neglectful. The world was well rid of her.

Carmichael again felt the old exhilaration welling within her. It was indeed nice to know that Pearson was no longer in the world.

She thought of the flasher. Well, of course, that coincidence was almost too good to be true. She doubted now if they'd ever catch him, for when he heard that there'd been a murder outside the nurses' home, as he was bound to, he was hardly likely to come back. Yes, on the whole, that was very convenient, but then things usually were convenient for her, Carmichael thought smugly.

One little thing, however, worried her. Supposing they traced the purchase of the tie back to her? Oh, surely they couldn't do that, not easily. Just a women going in to buy a tie in a great store like that. It could have been the flasher's girlfriend or even his sister. No, she didn't think that would come up at all. The tie was bought by a woman, well, even if the shop assistant remembered that, they'd probably sold far more than one tie that morning. There was the girl at the cash desk, but as far as

Carmichael could remember she hadn't even looked up at her. She didn't think the tie was of any consequence. She would deal with it if it arose. The police were clever, they could trace things back to . . . but trace it to her? She doubted it. No, she felt things would go quite smoothly, especially with such a wonderful suspect as the flasher. Her repugnance for him vanished. He was really a very useful member of society now. After all, flashing, he hardly harmed anybody, didn't harm a patient anyway. She smiled to herself and called to Sister Taylor who was just coming on duty.

'I'm off to lunch, Sister,' and as an afterthought added, 'Did you enjoy yourself last night?'

Sister Taylor looked up sharply and blushed. 'Yes, we did, how did you know?'

'I was there with Derek,' said Carmichael selfconsciously. 'I hope you don't mind my mentioning it, I just thought . . .'

'Oh no, no, of course not. Nigel and I like Hatchers End, don't you? It's not too far out and is very pleasant.'

'Yes, we do like it, we're thinking of having dinner there sometime soon. We haven't so far, but we hear it's very good, the food I mean,' said Carmichael airily.

The eyes of the two women met and Carmichael sensed a fellow feeling with another female that she had never felt before. It gave her a sense of intense triumph as she turned away. What she had got was worth fighting for, worth killing for.

She told Sister Taylor briefly about the death of Nurse Pearson, and of the gardener's boy finding her. Sister Taylor expressed all the horror that she felt and seemed genuinely upset.

'The flasher, that awful man. I didn't know he'd turn out to be a murderer,' said Taylor.

Carmichael nodded sagely and walked out of the department, aware that her junior sister was still gazing after her with a look of horror on her face. But it was not that, not that expression that Carmichael carried with her out of the department, no, it was that earlier look, that look of fellow feeling that had passed between them when she had mentioned Derek. As to her remark about the flasher . . . well, of course, she was so right, who would ever have thought that he would turn out to be a murderer?

17

In spite of the fact that the complex was so large and scattered, the news of the finding of a murdered nurse in the hospital grounds spread like a bush fire through the hospital.

When Carmichael arrived in the lunch room, the sisters, the cleaners, the canteen staff and the medical staff were all talking about the killing, speculating and making wild guesses. This certainly would last a little longer than the usual storm in a teacup. Carmichael said little but listened carefully.

Almost without exception the Peeping Tom, the flasher, or whatever he was called, was blamed.

'The police should have caught him.' 'The police should have been more diligent.' 'There should have been more of them.' 'They should have patrolled all night.' 'They just thought that because it was a nurses' home and there usually was a Peeping Tom around that it could be left.' So went the remarks. There was regret, horror, fear, all sorts of emotions were expressed and Carmichael just listened. She did not hear anyone sound particularly sympathetic towards the dead nurse and she drew from this the conclusion that Debbie Pearson had not been particularly liked, at least not by any of the sisters.

'She was a very insolent, saucy woman,' one sister said. 'I had her on my ward for some time and I had to tell her off once or twice for being cheeky to visitors. Still, I wouldn't have wished this on her, I wouldn't have wished it on anybody – strangled, wasn't she?'

Carmichael looked up quickly, 'Did you find her kind to the patients?' she asked, breaking her long silence.

The sister nodded absently but another chimed in, the geriatric ward sister, Elizabeth Chalmers.

120

'She was quite nasty to some of my old dears. I reported her once, I found her slapping an old lady. No, I didn't like her. She always hurried the poor old things, but, as Sister Grimes said, I wouldn't wish this on anyone. I wonder what happened? I mean, was she raped? Has anything leaked out? I haven't heard a word except that she was taken straight to the mortuary. I saw one of the mortuary porters and he said she was soaking wet as if she'd been out there all night.'

'Did it rain last night?' asked a fat, rather sleepy-looking sister who reminded Carmichael of Jones.

'Did it rain! There was a thunderstorm as well for God's sake. You sleep like a dormouse,' said another sister and there was general laughter.

'Well, I tell you this,' said Sister O'Hara. 'I'm not going down that damn drive alone, I shall take my car, but then I've got to walk round from the garage I suppose. I don't know what to do. I guess I'll make a point of going to the home with someone every evening. That's the only way. It's a damn nuisance.'

The theatre sister, a blonde, rather heavily made-up woman who hadn't spoken till now said, 'I shall get my boyfriend to take me down each evening. If he hasn't got the car and he hasn't always got it, he'll have to walk me to the door that's all. I've only known him a little while and it's a lot to ask, but I'm jolly well not going down there alone. If he doesn't like it, well I won't go out with him,' and she banged her knife and fork down noisily on her plate.

'Perhaps he's the murderer, your boyfriend,' remarked one of the other sisters. 'He might be the flasher even, we don't know who the flasher is you know, it might be someone we know quite well, a doctor perhaps.'

'Oh no it isn't,' said Sister Grimes, the children's ward sister. 'Carmichael's seen him, seen his face quite close to and it wasn't anyone you know, was it, Carmichael?'

Carmichael looked up at her with eyes narrowed. 'I really couldn't tell you,' she said. 'His face was sort of distorted, he pressed it against the glass of my window if you remember.'

'But you've seen him again, you've seen him since, you saw him when you were with . . . you said.'

'Yes I did, I did see him again but I still wouldn't recognize

121

him, not if he was put in an identification parade or I saw a photograph, I really wouldn't. You don't look at their faces you know.' There was a general roar of laughter and Carmichael flushed. She had not meant that, she had not meant that she had concentrated on any other part of his anatomy and she was quick to say so.

'You misunderstood me, I mean you're so upset at the time that you don't take in their features, you don't register what they look like. You know perfectly well what I mean.' She got up. She had finished her meal and she wanted to be rid of them. She was walking out of the room but she heard the conversation that went on behind her as it so often did when she was leaving the room. She stopped, her back to the sisters, in order to hear the rest of the chatter.

'God, she's touchy, isn't she, old Carmichael. Still I suppose you can understand it, she's had two frights and it is her nurse who's gone . . . you know, dead. She worked on Casualty, Pearson did, she was a nasty little piece of work though, nasty woman, couldn't take to her at all. After the men she was, oh yes, I know that one, any man. Someone said she was married but I don't believe it, she was after anybody who'd have her, easy lay I'd say.'

'How old was she then?' the blonde sister asked with some curiosity.

'Couldn't tell you – thirty-five, perhaps more, could have been more, made up a bit, a bit of a tart really.'

'Don't speak ill of the dead,' said someone and the conversation ended abruptly.

That evening Carmichael was meeting Derek who was calling for her as usual at the home. She had not seen him all day and she wondered what his reaction would be. She imagined he would be pretty shocked. She half expected him to come to the department to speak to her about it, but that, she felt, would be a give-away for him. Obviously he wouldn't want her to think that he had anything whatever to do with Nurse Pearson.

Carmichael went off duty and changed into one of her nicest frocks, put on her perfume, made up her face and came out to meet him at six o'clock. It was a sunny evening and Carmichael paused on the home steps and watched Derek drumming his fingers on the steering wheel. He had given his usual small toot to let her know he was there – he did not always come in and knock on her door. This evening he did not look up, or get out and open the door for her. She noticed this but excused it as she felt his mind must be in some turmoil. She slipped into the seat beside him and banged the door firmly. He looked even more pale and drawn than the night before and Carmichael felt she must open the conversation about the dead girl.

'Awful happening, isn't it?' she said quickly. He looked at her absently and Carmichael noticed that the collar of his shirt showed a faint line round it – he was not as fresh and immaculate as usual.

'Dreadful,' he said, then realized that perhaps he had jumped too quickly to the obvious conclusion so he qualified it by saying, 'I suppose you mean the death of that nurse?'

'That nurse? I thought you knew her. You've spoken to her in Casualty, haven't you?'

He looked at her speculatively, his eyes veiled. He put up a hand to smooth his slightly ruffled hair.

'Have I? I don't remember. Pearson her name was, wasn't it?'

You liar, thought Carmichael complacently, but what else can you do but lie, after all, you must be feeling pretty grim. She looked down to hide her expression from him.

'Never mind. It's been talked of enough today. Where shall we go?'

He mentioned the Hatchery again but this time for dinner and she agreed. It was an expensive place, but she did not feel in the mood that evening to point that out and suggest somewhere cheaper. She felt he had to pay, and money would do for a start.

He started the car without his customary swift caress and they drove in silence along the road for some time. Carmichael cast covert glances at him now and again. At last, when she had made up her mind to do so, she spoke.

'You seem very down, very preoccupied, is it on account of this dead woman?' she asked.

Derek almost shook himself as if to get rid of his preoccupation and smiled at her apologetically.

123

'No, no of course not. I am a bit concerned, as you say, well, I've had one or two problems with the fire exit doors and it's on my mind a bit. I'm so sorry, Agnes.'

'Please don't apologize, I quite understand. Yours is a responsible job and I know how you must feel about it.'

They drove on but next time it was Derek Hanson who broke the silence.

'Will there be an autopsy on Nurse – Nurse Pearson?' he asked, gazing ahead of him at the road.

'Well, of course. She was murdered you know, she was strangled, of course there will be. Why do you ask?' Carmichael knew only too well why he was asking – the pregnancy of course. After all, he had an academic interest but that was all it was now, only academic, thanks to her.

'It was that bloody man, wasn't it? The flasher, I know it was. Not enough notice was taken about that man. He sounded as mad as a hatter and now he's proved it. Well, I hope they get him, hanging is too good for him. Thank goodness it will be a lifer if they catch him.' The unusual violence struck Carmichael as comic, but she nodded her head gravely

'Yes, indeed. The sisters were saying today that they don't think enough has been done about it. I don't think really there can be any doubt who it was.' But, as Derek nodded vigorously, she added, 'Unless of course the girl had a particular enemy, a boyfriend, someone who knew something about her, or she knew something about him. But I shouldn't think that's very likely.'

'What kind of girl was she, do you think?' Hanson asked and Carmichael noticed that he glanced at her long enough for the car to swerve dangerously.

'Keep your eyes on the road, Derek. It's not like you to drive like that.'

'I'm sorry,' he muttered and Carmichael saw his hand tighten on the wheel as she replied.

'She was a rather dreadful little woman really, common, very anxious to get married, after any man she could see. I was always telling her off for using too much make-up on duty, trying to flirt with the ambulance men and porters. She wasn't a good nurse either. She was reported on the geriatric ward for being cruel to the patients and I found her anything but sympathetic either to patients or relatives. I'm sorry to see this happen to her but she's no great loss to the hospital, indeed no loss at all. She was getting on too, you know, she was only an auxiliary and she was thirty-five or thirty-six at least.'

'Thirty-three.' The remark seemed to be wrung from Derek Hanson.

Carmichael looked at him quickly. 'Thirty-three? How do you know that? I thought you said you didn't know her at all, she certainly looked more than thirty-three.'

'Oh I . . .' Carmichael noticed that Derek's neck had reddened. 'One of the doctors told me, I think, I can't be sure, it could have been a porter.'

'Well, I should have thought she was older than that – thirty-six or thirty-seven probably, but then she wouldn't tell the truth, would she? I doubt whether that kind of woman would ever tell the truth about anything.'

'What do you mean?' This time Derek's eyes did not leave the road but Carmichael sensed a tenseness about him. She thought of the girl's remark about pregnancy and wondered if perhaps that could have been a lie. She must try and learn the result of the autopsy if she got the chance. If the girl hadn't been pregnant she would have killed her for nothing, but on the other hand Derek thought she was, so it was justified.

Derek became a bit more animated and they talked of other things. When they got to Hatchers End Carmichael noticed that he could not make up his mind what to order and said he was not feeling particularly hungry. Carmichael said the same so they had a small meal and then drove back to the nurses' home earlier than usual.

On the whole it had not been a particularly enjoyable evening. Derek Hanson had not been a very lively companion. When they said good night Derek put his arm along the back of Carmichael's seat, preparatory, she knew, to giving his usual chaste kiss.

She put her hand gently on his chest and stopped him and, looking him directly in the eye, said: 'What's the matter, Derek, you don't seem to be your usual self, you seem worried, distracted. It can't just be the fire doors – is something else upsetting you?'

Derek took a moment or two to reply and then said: 'Well it is. I feel worried, Agnes, about you and that flasher man and you living on the ground floor. Well, it worries me, that's all. If he can do that to one girl he can do it to another and I'm deeply worried for you.'

Carmichael kept her eyes fixed on his; his were the first to drop. She knew that what he said was a complete falsehood, he was not bothered about her being attacked, he was just worried about Nurse Pearson, the murder, that's what was worrying him. He's a quick thinker, she thought, with some admiration. Still, she reacted as she knew he hoped she would.

'How very thoughtful of you, Derek. But you're not to worry. I shall keep my window firmly locked and I'm sure the police now will be very vigilant. They say there's one man patrolling the grounds all night with a dog and there's someone posted at the scene of the crime, so please don't worry. It's different now, you know, a murder has been committed, whether it's that man or not they won't leave it, they won't just leave it and go away.'

She would have to see that no harm ever came to Derek. He was obviously not to be trusted and, more particularly, he could not trust himself. Suddenly Carmichael felt more protective than ever towards him. He was a liar and he could not be trusted with women or money. But what did that matter? He had her, Carmichael, to protect him from all these hazards.

She got out of the car, but he hadn't moved as usual to rush round and open the door for her. As she stepped out he said, 'Oh, I'm sorry, Agnes, darling, I'm forgetting my manners.'

'Don't worry – don't worry – don't worry. How many times have I said that to you this evening?' Carmichael felt so easy, so relaxed. His maleness and her femaleness seemed to be fused together in one person. It was as if already they had slept together. She felt strange, it was probably a kind of intercourse that he didn't understand at all – but she did. She put her hand in the car and very gently stroked his face.

'Good night, Derek. See you tomorrow,' she said gently.

He looked at her and nodded dumbly. 'Yes, of course, of course, Agnes,' he said.

Carmichael left him and went into the home, pushing the heavy glass door open with confidence. The flasher? Yes, the nurses must certainly look out for him, though she very much doubted if after this he would ever come near the place again. It would be, as she had said to Derek, policed carefully. They would not leave the nurses unguarded, unprotected, now. Well, good would come of her act, she thought, as she went across to her own room. Pearson was no longer a problem to the patients, to Derek or to her or to her department and because of her death the flasher would be kept at bay too.

Carmichael opened the door. Her window was open. She went over, closed and locked it and pulled the curtain across. It was a dark night outside but everything, everything was going to be perfect. Marriage, a man of her own. She remembered Tony the gardener that morning, it seemed a long time ago. Poor boy what a shock.

She went about her usual routine when getting ready for bed. She felt smug and when at last she switched out the light she thought: Pearson, what a nasty woman. Pearson would probably be the last. After all, respectable married women don't do that kind of thing. Carmichael remembered again the fleshy feeling of the woman's neck, the tightening tie, the bulging eyes, the lipsticked mouth hanging slightly open. There was a certain amount of regret behind the feeling that never again, never again would she need to . . . After all she would be safely married, a wife, and this kind of situation would not arise. Wives just didn't do these things.

She got into bed, pulled the sheet up to her neck, turned over and made the pillow comfortable under her head. She thought again of the murdered woman but this time without fear. No imagined bump on the glass of her window and no bad dream disturbed her.

18

The murder inquiry proceeded as murder inquiries do, seemingly slowly, apparently without solving anything, though the room they had set up in the hospital was never empty and the telephones installed in it were constantly ringing, as Carmichael knew, from her visit to the inquiry room when she had told the inspector all she knew about the flasher and Auxiliary Nurse Pearson.

She had felt no nervousness when she went in. Inspector Murphy, a tall, dark Irishman, had greeted her with kindness and courtesy. She felt her sister's uniform made his manner slightly more deferential.

'Tell me, Sister, did you know Nurse Pearson well?' he had asked.

'No, not particularly well. She was just a nurse in my department and had been for two months . . .' Carmichael had tailed off but she obviously had more to say.

The detective arched his eyebrows slightly and tapped his teeth with the end of his pencil. 'A good nurse, a happy, contented sort of girl?'

'Girl, I would hardly call her that,' Carmichael had said and then regretted it, it sounded catty, but she went on: 'Yes, I would say she was happy enough, but not a particularly good nurse, I had to reprimand her several times, not a good time-keeper and she was not very nice to patients or relatives, but I suppose in these days she was adequate.' If Carmichael's tone had surprised him, his arched eyebrows were the only manifestation of this.

He continued, 'Did you know anything about her social life . . . boyfriends?'

Carmichael had shaken her head very decidedly. 'Oh no, no. She was apt to be rather . . . what can I say . . . familiar with men, ambulance drivers, porters and so on, but I didn't know of a steady boyfriend. She sometimes talked to my nurses about going out in the evening and that may have involved a man friend, but I really don't know.'

'That is the line, of course you must realize, sister, we are pursuing. We want to get in touch with all the murdered woman's men friends and it is important, if you have any recollection of somebody visiting her in the Casualty department or of her phoning anyone, if you have perhaps heard her mention a name, for you to tell us.'

'I do not allow my nurses to receive or make private telephone calls. If they wish to do so they must ask me for permission to leave the department and go to the public phones in the front hall. As to visitors, most certainly not. No nurse of mine would be visited by anyone while in the Casualty department, of that I do assure you.'

Carmichael saw a sly glance pass between the detective inspector and a policeman sitting at a desk a few feet away, typing busily. He then looked back at her gravely.

'Well, I am sure that is how a department like yours would be run, Sister Carmichael.' She bridled. 'But of course it might be possible for a young man to slip in some time when you're not there, have you by any chance heard your junior sister, Sister Taylor, speak of anyone who came to see Nurse Pearson?'

Carmichael had shaken her head rather contemptuously and replied: 'I assure you I know exactly what is going on in my department when I am there and when I am absent, particularly with regard to Auxiliary Nurse Pearson.'

That had ended the interview. Carmichael had come out feeling triumphant, yet vaguely bored. It had all happened before and she knew the routine. This time the questions, the investigation seemed rather unreal to Carmichael as if it was taking place on the television screen and she was watching with detached interest. At any moment she could switch it off if she wished and have just a blank screen to look at, no thoughts, nothing. She didn'tr altogether like this feeling, it related somehow to her stay in the psychiatric hospital. She was not depressed, however – perhaps elated would be the word and yet she didn't trust that feeling either.

The next time she was called back into the interview room to talk to Inspector Murphy he again wanted her to tell them what she knew about Debbie Pearson's character. Why they should think that she should know so much, or indeed anything Carmichael could not quite understand. They wanted to know everything of Pearson's background too, and Carmichael wondered why they asked her these questions. Surely the woman had relatives,

As Carmichael came out of the interview room for the second time, she met Derek going in. They had not met for two evenings but Carmichael was seeing him that night. He stopped to let her pass through the door and smiled at her. His smile was wintry, nervous, not his usual wide, confident smile. Impulsively Carmichael put out her hand and he grasped it almost as if he was shaking hands. She let the hand go and it dropped limply to his side.

'See you tonight,' she said. He nodded almost absent-mindedly.

'I'll be there, 6.30 we said, didn't we?'

Carmichael nodded and walked away and left him to go into the room. As she did so she wondered what questions they would ask him. Indeed, she was rather dismayed that he was being asked anything. Why and how did they connect him with Pearson's murder or with Pearson in any way? Could someone have seen them and told the inspector that they had been out together one evening perhaps? It could be. Carmichael's heart beat a little quicker as she made her way back to her department. She must wait till tonight, wait until she could question him, which she would do, closely. If he needed protection she would give it to him. She wondered who it was who had seen them. A nurse, a porter, a doctor? Someone must have seen him somewhere with Pearson for the inspector to send for him, surely? Well, these things got around no matter how you tried to conceal them, Carmichael thought.

For the rest of the day Carmichael lost her elation. She felt apprehensive and almost as nervous as Derek had looked as he went through that door to be questioned.

She was determined that when she went to lunch she would listen more closely to what the others were saying, listen to them gossiping about the murder inquiry. Perhaps they might have heard something which would connect Derek with the girl. She was a little late for lunch because half an hour before two small children had been brought in, a brother and sister, three and four years old. According to their mother they had eaten a bottle of junior aspirin. Carmichael had stayed to supervise the stomach wash-outs herself. The little boy who had kept his mouth firmly closed when asked again and again by his wailing mother: 'Did you eat the sweeties' was found to have eaten none, but when the little girl's stomach was washed out the tablets came pouring out. It was a satisfying thing for any nurse, Carmichael thought, momentarily forgetting Derek and her own problems. The nurses had looked at her in admiration.

'You were right, Sister,' one said, 'you thought all along it was the little girl.'

'I wasn't absolutely sure, nurse,' she said benignly, 'though doctor did lean towards the little boy. He thought he looked sleepy, but somehow I didn't think so.'

The doctor who had ordered the little boy to have his stomach washed out first looked slightly sheepish and walked out of the theatre to talk to the mother. Carmichael smiled and also walked out, feeling rather God-like and knowing. She could feel the nurses' respectful glances as she went.

The two children had been difficult. They had had to roll them up in blankets and put them on the table like little bundles to wash out their stomachs.

'Poor kids,' said one of the nurses.

'Poor kids indeed, but poorer if they die of it. This is one time, nurse, when I agree with wrapping a child in a blanket, and pinioning the arms so that one can wash a poison out. After all, if we lost either of these two what a disgrace it would be!' She was conscious that perhaps she had used the wrong word, maybe a better word would have been 'tragedy' not 'disgrace', but it was said now and the look of admiration did not leave her nurses' faces.

At lunch Carmichael listened carefully as she had intended to what the sisters said. The main topic of conversation was, as might be expected, Debbie Pearson. There were plenty of rumours. A man looking very like the flasher had been seen just a few minutes before the murder. He had been running away from the scene of the crime, overcoat open, showing a white shirt without a tie. Another man had been seen in a white coat walking that way before Debbie Pearson had gone off duty, and so on. Carmichael listened and listened, but nothing was said about Derek until right at the end of lunch. Carmichael, who usually did not have a sweet, had decided on this occasion to have one. And suddenly, just as she was finishing her *bombe surprise*, one of the sisters began again.

'Well, they're questioning everybody, they're trying to find out who her boyfriends were, I mean among the hospital personnel. She did go out with that porter, you know, Bob what's-his-name, but he didn't know anything about it. Lucky for him he had an alibi apparently.'

Carmichael marvelled about how the sisters managed to get these details, but get them they did.

'Oh, yeah, and there's the fire officer, Derek who's-it, you know. He's been questioned. A nurse on my ward saw them together one night. They were out somewhere, I can't remember where, in a pub, I believe, but I've forgotten, I can't be sure. But she saw them all right.'

There was an awkward silence. Some of the sisters knew that Carmichael was going out with the fire officer. She rose without glancing at anyone and walked out of the room. Silence followed her.

So someone had seen him, but who? A nurse on that sister's ward. She screwed her eyes up in concentration. Yes, she was junior sister on the women's surgical, it was a big ward, who could it have been? There were lots of nurses and she wished she had stayed a little longer to see if the girl's name would come up. She should not have left so abruptly, but that silence had been so embarrassing. They didn't understand, they simply didn't understand, that she and Derek had an arrangement, an understanding that blotted out everything. Such a handsome man was bound to have affairs. Still, she wished she'd heard the name of the girl. She would look at the rota and see what names were on it for that ward. That would narrow it down to about

132

fifteen or sixteen nurses, but even so it would be difficult. She almost turned to go back, then decided against it and made her way up to her office, hoping that the sisters would follow her and keep up their chat about the 'Death in the garden', as it was being called in the papers.

She poured herself out coffee and after a few minutes some of the sisters drifted in. But they started talking about quite different things and the television was switched on in order to catch the last of the midday news. Although Carmichael sat it out until they began to leave she heard no more and was disappointed. The only other way to find out was to ask Derek directly that evening, ask him outright if he knew who had seen him with Nurse Pearson. He would have to tell her the truth, he was worried enough, she was sure, and he wouldn't prevaricate. Yes, that's what she would do.

The rest of the afternoon was not particularly busy, there were just the usual small casualties. A man with an acute attack of asthma gave them some anxiety but he was given some cortisone and then, since he was determined not to be admitted, was taken home by ambulance. Carmichael was not happy with this arrangement but as the patient refused to come in there was nothing they could do. She was sure he was very used to his asthma attacks and had a wife at home whom she telephoned before letting him go. Having got the wife's assurance that she would look after him Carmichael had had to be satisfied.

At last six o'clock came. Carmichael could leave her department and go over to the nurses' home and get ready for her evening out, an evening which, in a way, she was rather dreading because she felt somehow that Derek would tell her what was worrying him and then the burden would rest on her shoulders to do something about it. Well, she would, she always did, and after all she would have to do it for the rest of her life. She would always have to look after him, he was weak, she knew that, but rather someone weak than someone who would boss her about and make her do this and that. She couldn't bear that, she had been her own mistress too long.

She squared her shoulders and marched rather than walked to the nurses' home, debating what she should wear. The evenings were getting warmer so she would take her light

133

oatmeal coat out of its plastic bag and wear it this evening. Yes. She hoped it wouldn't smell musty, it had been in the wardrobe since last summer. Perhaps she would wear lighter shoes. She gave her mind to this problem as she walked back to the home and into her own room to dress.

19

Instead of sounding the car horn once, as he usually did, to let Carmichael know he was there, Derek came in and knocked on her door. When she opened it he asked with his usual politeness if he might come in. Carmichael, slightly surprised, said that he could. As he came in, she noticed his obvious agitation.

'What's the matter, Derek?' she asked, wondering if something had happened while he had been with Inspector Murphy, something about Nurse Pearson.

'I want you to do something for me and I simply don't know how to ask.' It was very like the beginning of the speech in which he had asked her for the money, Carmichael thought wryly. She wondered what favour he was going to ask this time.

'I was summoned to go into the police this morning, their inquiry room. I had to go to be interviewed. You know that plain-clothes chap, the Irish one, he was there.'

'Yes, you were going in as I came out, weren't you, Derek?' Carmichael said.

'Oh, yes, of course, I'd forgotten. Did they ask you any . . . anything . . .?'

'No. He only asked me if I knew any of Nurse Pearson's boyfriends and I said I didn't, then he suggested that I might have seen them if they had come to the Casualty department to visit her. I put him in his place pretty quickly about that I can assure you. The idea of boyfriends coming to visit my nurses in my department. That's something I would not allow. And you – what did he ask you? It seems to have worried you considerably.'

'Oh, it's not that, it's not that at all, they only asked me routine things. Did I know her, had I seen her about and so on.

I felt there was something underlying their questions maybe I was wrong. But I got a shock, Agnes, I really did.'

Carmichael inclined her head attentively and sat down in a chair opposite him and waited. She motioned him to be seated.

'Do you know a girl called Merrill, Rosie Merill? She's a pupil nurse, I think you call her, not a staff nurse yet. She's a vixenish little thing, I've known her for some time. Well, not her, I know her father actually. He was a fireman at one time but left and for some reason she doesn't seem to like me, I don't know why. Anyway, she's trying to blackmail me, Agnes, in a way, a pretty inexpert way but the fact remains she is.'

'Blackmailing you? How can she? What can she possibly know about you that she can blackmail you about?' Though Carmichael said this, in her heart she guessed what the girl knew, and as Derek Hanson continued she found she was right.

'Oh, she knows, she knows about Debbie Pearson and me. I knew Debbie, Agnes, long before I came here. She was always promiscuous and well, we did go out together quite a bit. This girl Rosie was quite a friend of Debbie's at the time and she knew about us. She even came out with us once, with another man, made up a foursome. I'd forgotten it, forgotten all about it, can't even remember the man's name now. Then, before I came here I broke it off very firmly with Debbie, I didn't want anything more to do with her.'

'It's a pity you had anything to do with her in the first place, Derek,' said Carmichael, coldly.

The coldness in her voice seemed to upset Derek Hanson, for he said urgently: 'Agnes, it was all over long before I came here, but Rosie's a trouble-maker, always has been. I think she feels there's something in it for her. I borrowed some money from Debbie, oh, ages ago, and I was going to pay it back . . .'

'Out of my two thousand pounds?' asked Carmichael ironically.

'Oh no, not that, I wanted that for a totally different purpose, I told you that. No, I was going to pay her back but I hadn't got around to it, that's all. This girl knew about it. I suppose they chatted and Debbie told her. She, Rosie, was very unpleasant. She said, as I hadn't paid Debbie, perhaps I could pay her or she might decide to go to the police and tell them how long

Debbie and I had been going out together.'

'Does anyone else know, Derek?' Carmichael asked. She felt very calm, very calm indeed. This was a situation that she could cope with, she thought.

'No, I don't think so. We never went out together anywhere near here. We usually went to a road house a long way away.'

'Why was that? Why didn't you want to be seen?' queried Carmichael.

'Well I . . .' Derek Hanson stumbled a little, 'I didn't want to be seen with her, that's all, she wasn't my type of woman. A man has needs, you know that, Agnes, and well . . . when I met you I felt quite differently, you know that.' He looked at her directly and Carmichael's heart melted. She knew she would stand by him through thick and thin, before and after they were married. That was the price she would have to pay for being married. He was weak and he was a liar. Saying that he'd given up Debbie Pearson long before he'd come to Hemmington General – that was a lie.

'I still don't quite see . . . of course, you can't give her any money . . . but suppose she does tell the police you knew Debbie, that doesn't mean anything.'

'Well, it does and it doesn't. Suppose they ask me where I was that night, the night she was killed, I mean.'

'You were at the meeting, you didn't get to me until quarter to ten, you know you didn't.' Derek Hanson looked completely wretched – as well he might, thought Carmichael.

'I met Debbie Pearson that night, she made me, she rang me up, she wanted her money and I did meet her. I met her in the grounds where she was killed. But she was alive, Agnes, she was alive when I left her, I can swear to that. I would swear to it on anything you hold dear. If you've got a Bible, I'll . . .'

'There's no need for drama, Derek, I'm sure you didn't kill the woman, I don't think you're that kind of person.' Carmichael knew that no one in the world could be as sure that he hadn't killed Debbie Pearson as she was, and the thought filled her with a rare humour.

'Don't worry, Derek, what do you want me to do about it?'

'Well, if you would say I was with you from the time the meeting really packed up, that was about quarter past eight, if you would say I was with you all the time, that we were in here in your room and then we went out, that's an hour and a half, and that's when she was killed, isn't it?'

Carmichael nodded. 'I believe so. Well, that should be quite easy, if the occasion arises I will certainly tell them that.'

'There's another little problem too. When I came down to see her, that awful bitch, I didn't come by car, I walked. I didn't want anyone to see my car outside. So how can we get round that?

Again amusement struck Carmichael. This man was almost entirely dependent on her. She could do what she liked with him. Marriage now would be so easy. She smiled reassuringly and leaned forward clasping his hand, which was icy cold.

'Don't worry, we can make some excuse for that if it comes up, which I doubt. We can say you walked down to the home because you wanted some exercise, stayed with me for a time and then went and fetched the car. I doubt if anyone would have noticed whether it was there or not. It's a chance and we'll have to take it.'

Carmichael felt a bubble of laughter almost rise in her. She had a hysterical wish to giggle which she crushed sternly.

'Well, now all that's arranged, shall we go out? Think no more about this girl, what's her name? Merrill.'

As Carmichael slipped into her coat she thought of the conversation at lunch that day and of the surgical ward sister's remark. Now she had no need to find out who the nurse was who had spoken about Derek Hanson and Debbie. It had all fallen nicely into her lap as usual. It really meant nothing, what the girl had said, even if the sisters knew it. So he had been out with Debbie Pearson – who hadn't? As long as he had an alibi for the time, that was really all that mattered. She was smiling and looked so relaxed that Derek Hanson's spirits seemed to revive a little.

'Oh, Agnes, you're such a comfort,' he said. He came forward and put his arms round her, holding her tightly for a moment, not kissing her, but with his cheek resting against hers. Carmichael gazed out of the window, motionless, not returning his caress. Had Derek Hanson been able to observe her eyes as they gazed through the window, he would have

138

wondered . . . Resolve seemed to stiffen her, she would look after him. He was like a baby. Who was it said that all men were little boys at heart? It was true, that's all he was. Still, most husbands were similar, she imagined.

'Come along, Derek,' she said, a kindly tone in her voice. 'Come along, dear. We'll go out and have a good, stiff drink, that's what you want and probably I do as well.'

She preceded him out of the door to the waiting car. They both got in and almost tenderly Derek leaned over and pulled out the strap for her and buckled her in.

'I really don't know what I'd do without you, Agnes,' he said with a touch of his usual pompousness and over-gallantry.

Carmichael looked at him. The light from the lamp illuminated the interior of the car, and she gazed at him rather affectionately.

'Don't worry, Derek,' she said. 'You won't have to do without me.'

She turned back as Derek slid the car into gear and they set out for their evening together. Carmichael did not look at him again until they arrived at the restaurant where they were going to have dinner. It was a new place Derek had heard of and thought they would try, and Carmichael had acquiesced absent-mindedly.

The Swan was quite different from Hatchers End, more countrified, with beams that might, or might not, be the original ones and horse brasses; a small bar compared with the one at Hatchers End. It was intimate and quiet. As they entered Carmichael got the feeling that she was surrounded by the country which was, of course, the impression they wished to give. She realized this and found it very pleasant. The furniture, well waxed, shone in the dull lighting. There was even a log fire burning, though the evening was warm.

'What a nice place, Derek,' she said with appreciation, but Derek hardly answered her, just nodded. His anxiety was closing in on him again, Carmichael thought.

She chose the table at which she wanted to sit while they had their drinks and seated herself in a low chair, watching Derek as he went to the bar. In a way, she thought, it was a new Derek, quite different from the Derek of even a week ago. She had always dreamed that if she were lucky enough to marry it would be to a man who could cope with everything, who would take over all the chores of living, like house insurance, mortgage, travelling, the car, everything, and she would just have the house to run. She had thought a man could manage his business affairs and his life and look after hers as well. She thought that had been what she had wanted, but she realized now as she watched Derek that this was not how it was going to be, she was the one with the strength. She half regretted this, yet she was not one who would like to lose her independence, she wouldn't want that to happen. Probably this, in a way, would be more satisfactory. She would always have, as it were, the edge on him.

Derek turned from the bar, a drink in each hand, and came over to the table. She could see by the colour of the liquid in the glasses that they were doubles and she gave him a quick, fleeting smile of thanks as he put them down. He eased himself down into the armchair next to hers and gazed round for a moment.

Two more people came in but did not sit near them. Derek turned to her and for the moment said nothing. They sipped their drinks. They were in a way, Carmichael thought, sizing each other up in the situation in which they found themselves. It was interesting.

'Thank you so much, Agnes, I knew I could rely on you. It's a nasty situation. I really don't know what to say, but I guess I haven't been any angel.'

Carmichael twirled the glass before her. The smell of the drink came up to her pleasantly and she thought in a detached way that she was beginning to like brandy. The glass twirled slowly in her hand, her fingers rotating the stem. For once Carmichael was not worrying about her looks, her make-up, her hair, anything about her appearance. She knew why, she felt that she had got Derek now, the fact that she had given him an alibi for the gruesome act that had happened outside the nurses' home had made her completely sure of him.

'You look sort of happy, well complacent about it all, Agnes,' Derek said, and Carmichael gave him credit for having more sensitivity than she had thought, since he had noticed her mood.

'Yes, I do feel quite happy, Derek, quite happy.'

Derek Hanson slipped his hand into hers and they sat hand in hand at the table drinking their brandy. The waiter suddenly appeared with the menu and put it down in front of them, glancing at their fingers and looking quickly away.

'I wonder what he thinks,' murmured Carmichael and then realized she didn't care what anyone thought any more. It was a very comfortable feeling. She thought of the building society passbook in her handbag, of the two thousand pounds which she was going to draw out. Well, she would do that now, there was no risk to her money, he was hers.

Involuntarily she squeezed his hand and he looked at her and squeezed her hand back. Carmichael felt no thrill and she was sure that he didn't either, but that didn't matter. They had an understanding and quite a different understanding from the one they had had at the beginning of the evening. Their conversation had sealed and settled it. Carmichael looked down again at her glass, but instead of her glass she saw Harry's face looking up at her, so different, but then Harry, Harry was an aristocrat, Harry was a gentleman. This man, well . . .

'What would you like to choose, Agnes?' Derek's voice broke in on her thoughts and she looked up at him, he was holding the menu so she could see it.

'Oh, you choose, I'm not very hungry,' she said.

20

Carmichael's protective attitude towards Derek Hanson continued, in fact it grew. His apprehension about what this nurse knew and how it would affect him seemed to feed Carmichael's confidence. She took the trouble to go up to the women's surgical ward to have a look at Nurse Merrill. To her surprise she was young and pretty, and, contrary to what Derek said, was already wearing her staff nurse's belt. Carmichael wondered briefly what the relationship between her and Derek had been, then dismissed the thought. She knew that as she grew more and more intimate with him and as their lives became more and more entwined she would find out a great many things about him which, if she allowed them to, could upset her. She was determined not to worry and so, having seen her, she dismissed the girl from her thoughts.

Agnes Carmichael was confident she could handle the situation. Derek's alibi would be quite watertight. She, a senior, responsible member of the staff, could vouch for him. If she said he had been with her from quarter past eight, that would be enough. Meanwhile, for the moment anyway, the Irish detective inspector did not send for Derek again.

The inquiry went on, and once when Carmichael, out of curiosity, had gone round to the scene of the crime, she had found it roped off with white nylon ribbon attached to metal poles. That, thought Carmichael wryly, was where the body had been found. She had read many detective novels and seen a lot of television plays in which chalk marks had indicated where the body had lain. In a way she would have liked to have seen some of the photographs they had taken but of course that was quite impossible.

A curious feeling was coming over Carmichael. It was not like the one that had led to her incarceration in the psychiatric ward. No, it was quite different. She felt that the life that stretched before her now was utterly alien to the one she had led before. There would be no more need to dispose of anyone. Although Derek Hanson was weak, nevertheless he would be a buffer between her and the rest of the world. She would be able to lean on him, ask his advice. It was really, she thought dreamily, rather like having him drive the car – he would in future drive her life. Oh, of course, she would actually be in charge, but to the outsider it would be Derek. She would have to see that he didn't do anything wrong, like driving with worn tyres, or without insurance, or with another woman in the car. She would have to keep an eye on him constantly, but there would be no need for any more violent action on her part and it made her feel relaxed, less nervous. She looked back to what she had done in the past, it had always been done for the best and that was comforting. She herself could now assume the role of a woman, just that, a woman with her own man; that was all she would be and all she wanted to be once they were married.

Madeleine Taylor and Nigel Denton announced their engagement and Carmichael was rather pleased when Madeleine Taylor came to her before the announcement was made and showed her her engagement ring.

'I want you to be the first to know, Agnes,' she said. It was friendly, it was warm and Carmichael was specially pleased when Madeleine added, 'I feel somehow you're going to be the next. I've just got this feeling. I'm sorry if I . . .' and she had blushed.

Carmichael credited her with tactfulness, niceness and she had replied with her eyes not meeting Madeleine Taylor's, 'Yes, you may be right. Congratulations, Madeleine, or I believe I shouldn't congratulate you I should congratulate Mr Denton, shouldn't I?'

Madeleine had laughed and put her hand on Carmichael's arm and squeezed it, almost with affection. Carmichael was totally unused to such manifestations of intimacy or fondness from another woman and she felt tears prick behind her eyes and had hastily suppressed them.

'Have you and Derek made any plans? Perhaps I shouldn't pry, I don't mean to but I can tell you are fond of him and he of you, the way he looks at you when he comes to the department, I mean. Of course, I've only seen you together here, in Casualty,' said Madeleine still flushed. Carmichael raised her eyes at last and looked straight at her junior sister. It was time to be open, she thought, time to tell the truth.

'Yes, we are very fond of each other,' she said almost shyly. 'We intend to . . . well, when all this has blown over and things are quieter.' Carmichael was well aware that the rumours about Derek being seen with Debbie Pearson must have got to her junior sister. 'Yes, we will announce our engagement.'

'Oh, I'm glad, so glad for you. When you're as happy as I am you want everyone else to be happy too. I suppose that's what they call wearing rose-tinted spectacles.'

Carmichael nodded and as she did so a sharp stab of fear went through her. Had she been too hasty? After all, Derek hadn't proposed yet, but he would, of course he would, it was only a question of time. As she had just said it was only a matter of waiting for all this to blow over. Obviously Madeleine could not be aware just how much had got to blow over, but still she would understand.

That morning in the department it was so cheerful. Now and again a glance would pass between her and Madeleine Taylor, an understanding, sympathetic, smiling glance, and at coffee time Carmichael asked her to come in and have it in her office and Madeleine agreed. Afterwards, when they were sitting there, Carmichael did wonder whether perhaps Madeleine would rather have gone up to the rest room to show off her ring to the other sisters, although she did not seem to show any reluctance at staying with Carmichael.

They talked of Madeleine's wedding, when the date would be, in which Registry Office. She said that, of course, Carmichael must come. She was going to have rather a big reception because of her mother and father, they wanted it and you know what parents are, she said. Carmichael had not known what they were, but she nodded sympathetically and felt for a moment her own complete lack of background.

Nigel Denton, too, was charming to her when he came down

to the department, realizing that his fiancée had told Carmichael of their engagement. He, too, came especially, Carmichael felt, to see her and talked so openly and in such a friendly way that Carmichael began to feel one of them. She was aware that had she not had a man herself, she would have hated Madeleine Taylor and Nigel Denton, but now she, too, wore the rose-coloured spectacles. She smiled to herself at the thought, and when Nigel Denton left the department she thought briefly about his previous wife. Was he remembering, was he haunted? She remembered the story more clearly now. He had backed his car accidentally into his wife and killed her. She thought of the terrible trauma he must have gone through at the time and wondered if it had faded, if it had left him. She hoped so.

Then she thought again of Harry and how she had felt when he and Margaret Tarrant had shown so obviously that they were the pair who would marry, that there was no place for Carmichael with him. Yes, that had faded but it still hurt, still hurt a little – and there were other things. Well, everyone had something in the past to regret, to hurt them, she thought. Perhaps even Madeleine: after all, she was divorced, and with a rush of good-will she hoped that Nigel would not think of his wife again, or, if he did, that it wouldn't hurt, that he would look into the future with his attractive bride, just as she, Carmichael, would with Derek. She would look forward, never backward. Everything they all had done, Madeleine too, was behind them and now a new life was opening. It was wonderful.

The two women, Carmichael and Madeleine Taylor, were brought even closer together that afternoon in Casualty. A young child was brought in who was having convulsions. One fit after another shook his small body. Everything in Casualty was mustered round to help the child, an air-way, breathing apparatus, injections, the senior consultant physician was summoned, but the child went on from one fit to another. Madeleine looked across at Carmichael, her eyes were almost imploring. The child was so young, only four years old. The distracted mother and father sat in the waiting room. The child frothed at the mouth and the back arched as each convulsion shook him and the small body was racked. As Carmichael

145

looked at the child's distorted face she realized that nothing was being felt, that the child was completely unconscious. That was something to be thankful for. She spoke reassuringly of the fact to Madeleine.

Carmichael worked expertly, quickly, doing everything that the doctors ordered, just as the other nurses did. They worked and worked. 'Status epilepticus' she heard the senior physician say almost helplessly and thought, they may know the name but the child is going to die. An hour and a half later they had to tell the parents that the child had not survived.

When at last the small body had been taken to the mortuary, Madeleine turned to Carmichael and said with tears in her eyes: 'Oh, God, those poor parents, suppose it had been mine and Nigel's.'

Carmichael shook her head sympathetically but she did not feel as moved as Madeleine. Why, she wondered. Perhaps because she herself was past child-bearing age and knew that Derek and she would never have children.

The consultant physician came and thanked her for what she had done before he left the department and his registrar went out to deal with the parents. Carmichael said to Madeleine: 'Perhaps you would rather . . .?' and Madeleine had nodded almost eagerly and followed him, wanting to comfort, wanting to put her arms round one of the parents, and she herself, thought Carmichael, would feel better as a result.

Carmichael sat in her office for a while and a nurse brought her a cup of tea, the customary placebo after such a death. Carmichael sipped it absently and realized that though her feelings were not as deep as Madeleine Taylor's she did not regret the fact, she did not want to be tortured by things she could do nothing about.

After a time her junior sister came back and the department resumed its usual routine. Sister Taylor went off duty, but Carmichael was on till 8.30. She was about to go to tea when the phone rang. She answered it mechanically. It was Nigel Denton, his voice sounded urgent, thought Carmichael, but not in the least flustered.

'Major disaster, Sister, I'm sure you will know the procedure. A hotel in the town, I don't know it, it's called the Regent. It's

146

badly burned, almost gutted I believe. Casualties number over twenty according to my informant. They should be with you within the next ten minutes. Will you get the department ready, issue instructions of course for the cupboards to be unlocked that need to be. You'll want plenty of plasma, Sister Carmichael.'

As always the use of her name pleased Carmichael and she felt an inner strength rising in her. She almost purred. She was sorry of course that such a thing had occurred, she said this to herself almost severely, she was sorry for the victims, but what a chance to prove her prowess – and a fire! She wondered if Derek Hanson would figure in this, would he as fire officer be . . .? No, she supposed not, it was entirely a Casualty affair, he was just a hospital administrator. She answered Nigel Denton with a certain warmth in her voice.

'I will have everything ready, sir,' she said. The 'sir' had slipped off her tongue almost by mistake and she regretted it because she felt Nigel and she – because of the engagement, well because of everything – were almost friends. She should not have said 'sir' but it had been automatic and as she put the phone down she dismissed it from her mind.

She called her nurses together, told them what was coming into the department and they all looked at each other in some excitement and fright. Carmichael summoned the ward clerk who came in quickly, infected by the feeling of urgency in the department.

'Yes, Sister,' she said. Carmichael gave her a brief outline of what was happening and a list of the people she must inform: the hospital secretary, the nursing officer, the theatre, the path lab., X-ray and the head porter. The girl went quickly back to the telephone. In the case of a major disaster the clerk would stay as long as she was wanted if she volunteered to do so.

Carmichael made a quick round of the department to see those casualties who had been dealt with and could go home before the burns started coming along. She had some experience of burns in that department but not, she thought, on this scale.

Nigel Denton walked in followed by Miss Haskins and his senior house officer, all white-coated and ready.

I've notified the other consultants. We may need – well, just anything according to where the burns are, I couldn't get much out of the ambulance people, but then you never can. It may not be as bad as we think, on the other hand it may be worse. Is there anyone in the department that we can see and get out?'

Carmichael motioned to one examination room where a woman with a twisted ankle was sitting and Nigel Denton nodded to Miss Haskins to go and cope with the case which had already been X-rayed. She hurried off.

Porters arrived with extra mattresses which they laid down on the floor between the couches in the big dressing room so that it could house at least twenty people, more if necessary. The examination rooms would be kept for those very badly burned if there were any who did not go straight to the ward.

Carmichael's eyes darted around as she ordered nurses to put all the necessary equipment and the ointments for dressings ready to hand. She was in her element and perhaps had never felt so happy in her life as when Nigel Denton turned to his senior house officer and said lightly, 'We needn't worry. Sister Carmichael knows how to cope with an emergency. We've done it before, haven't we, Sister?'

She looked at him and joy and warmth flooded over her, she was almost overwhelmed as she answered.

'Well, in a way, we have, sir.' The 'sir' had slipped out again but if Nigel Denton noticed it his expression did not show it for he smiled with friendliness and intimacy.

'Are you getting Madeleine back?' he asked.

Carmichael nodded. 'I've rung everyone that I think I should, Mr Denton. I'm getting my nurses back just in case they're needed, those I can get in touch with. I've informed Mr Stewart and Miss Thompson and she'll inform anyone in the nursing hierarchy that we should.'

'Right. Well, we can summon what consultants we need if there are any eyes, or internal injuries, we shall see. I hate burns,' he said suddenly and turned away as they heard the first wail of an ambulance at the Casualty door. It might be the first of the burns, but it might be nothing to do with the hotel fire at all, thought Carmichael.

As one of the nurses was gently assisting the patient with the

148

twisted ankle out to her car, Carmichael called: 'Just see if that is one of those we are expecting or something else when you've finished with that patient.'

The nurse looked back at her and continued, her arm round the woman's waist, to the door of the waiting room where the patient was joined by her husband. Together they made their slow way through the waiting room. Carmichael felt a slight impatience, she wanted the woman out of the way before anything unpleasant-looking came through the door. The nurse felt the same and was hurrying the woman a little. At last they disappeared through the far door of the waiting room and Carmichael breathed a sigh of relief. The ambulance bay was not where the cars were parked and Carmichael knew that the danger of the two meeting a bad case of burns coming in had gone.

For a moment or two nothing happened and they all seemed poised waiting for the worst. The ambulance entrance door suddenly opened and a harassed looking ambulance man walked in. He saw, and recognized, Nigel Denton.

'It's pretty bad, sir,' he said, 'pretty bad. They've got five fire engines there.'

'Wheel them in, we can cope,' said Nigel Denton and they stood there, a team, ready and waiting.

21

Carmichael had never felt more proud of being a nurse, of being surrounded by a team the nursing side of which she had helped to train, and which she controlled. It was a great feeling, and it was strange, she thought, that only about six weeks ago, after a fire drill, she had hung up a chart and diagram that had been sent to her by a pharmaceutical firm and given all her nurses a long talk on burns.

As if reading her thoughts, one of her junior nurses passing her said, 'I remember what you said, Sister, in that talk you gave us. Lucky, wasn't it?'

She walked on and Carmichael forbore to say what rose quickly to her tongue – lucky is hardly the word for the people who are burned. Indeed she was glad she didn't say it for the animation and thankfulness on the nurse's face made her seem even better.

Apparently, from what Carmichael learned, the Regent Hotel had been rather busier than usual owing to the fact that the next day there was an agricultural show. Quite a number of people from outlying towns had come to spend the night there in order to have a full day at the show.

In all there were about sixteen people needing urgent care and many others with minor burns and injuries, some due not to the fire but to their hasty retreat from the hotel. All this Carmichael learned as she busied herself about her work. Four patients with charred limbs that might well have to be amputated had to be taken immediately to the ward. There was nothing one could do for them in Casualty except put up a plasma drip and see them safely up to the ward. In one case the man's trousers had been burned and pieces of the cloth remained in the charred tissue of the legs. This man would have to have an anaesthetic and his wounds dealt with while he was unconscious.

Some of the patients were given morphine on site, but those were the most badly hurt. Others were given it in the department under the close supervision of Miss Thompson who had donned a plastic apron and put herself as it were in a junior position to Carmichael. She made this very clear, saying: 'I don't want to take over, Carmichael, I just want to be here to help, so tell me what to do.'

Carmichael was grateful. In spite of the fact that she had called her off-duty nurses back, those that she could contact, and Madeleine Taylor was there, she needed all the help she could get.

Madeleine's face was flushed and her eyes worried. She looked, thought Carmichael without rancour, more attractive than ever. She saw that occasionally Nigel Denton glanced across at her and a look seemed to pass between them. Carmichael hoped that one day similar glances would pass between Derek and herself. She felt suddenly nearer to him because she was treating burns, because she was seeing what he must have seen so often as a fireman and later as fire chief. The thought warmed her too. It won't be long, she thought, it won't be long before we are irrevocably linked and then I won't have to worry. I won't have to worry if he borrows my money, chases other women or anything else. The thought retreated to the back of her mind when the next batch of burns came in, but it was there, glowing softly and comfortingly.

There was one woman whose eye was so badly burned that the ophthalmologist had to be called. He examined her eyes as best he could and turned to Carmichael and said: 'Admit.'

He then walked up to Nigel Denton to ask him if there were any more eye cases and when Denton shook his head he left the department, taciturn and silent as always. Carmichael, knowing that the ophthalmologist's manner would be hardly reassuring, went to see the woman when he had left. She told her that she would be admitted to the eye ward and that her family would be informed.

The Casualty clerk had exceeded all Carmichael's expectations. She could have gone at five o'clock. There was nothing in the major disaster instructions about the ward clerk. Carmichael watched her going from one patient to another, filling in the Casualty cards neatly and having the sense to take with her a clip board on which to rest them. Carmichael gave her full marks and said so once as she met her crossing from a cubicle to her office.

'Well done, Janice. I like the way you're doing things, the clipboard is a help too. Did you have it all ready?'

The girl looked at her shyly. 'Well, I thought if anything like this did happen I'd want to stay and do what I could. It's just a little thing you know, putting things down on your knee is difficult.' She had flushed rosily and Carmichael had felt real pleasure at being able to approve the girl's actions.

The more Carmichael worked the more warmth she seemed to give out. Even her staff, busy as they were, noticed it and the doctors too. She heard Dr Singh say to Miss Haskins: 'It brings out the best in our sister, a crisis, doesn't it? She was almost nice to me just now.' He laughed, entirely taking the sting out of the remark and Carmichael made a little grimace and thought that perhaps she hadn't been all that nice to Dr Singh and would try to do better in the future.

At last she could pause for a moment. She got the porters to take away the unused mattresses. This gave them more space in which to move, and the department began to assume its usual tidy look as the nurses finished the small wounds of the patients in the dressing room and got ready to bring in more from the waiting room.

Carmichael went through to see how many were left. There were at least twenty people sitting there. Carmichael glanced at her watch and saw it was nine o'clock. She had had no idea it was so late, the time had gone by so rapidly. Nine o'clock. Well, Derek would know where she was, he would not wait she was sure, she did not expect him to. They would meet tomorrow. He would telephone her, she felt absolutely sure, quite satisfied that that was what he would do. He would know the importance of an emergency like this.

She called in four more cases and sat them down next to the beds in the big dressing room and asked Madeleine Taylor if she would like to go off duty. The girl looked up from a dressing she was doing and pushed her hair back with her wrist.

'Shan't be sorry to get off, Sister,' she said, 'but there's no hurry. How many more have we got out there?'

'About sixteen,' said Carmichael. 'But they only look like minor things, minor burns. I can cope with them, and now the night staff is on we can begin to let the nurses go off.'

'You haven't had as much off duty as I have. No, I'll stay till we've cleared them all.'

Carmichael nodded and went back into the waiting room. As she did so the far door opened and a fireman came in with a slightly apologetic air. Carmichael went forward quickly to greet him, he brought an even more pungent smell of burning in with him.

'What have you done, have you burnt yourself, have you got burns anywhere?' she asked. 'Is the smoke troubling you?' They had had two cases of firemen overcome by smoke and their coughing had been horrendous, but this man was not coughing, he was just standing there holding one hand in the other, a piece of lint across the back of his left hand. He held the hand out to Carmichael, removed the lint and showed her quite a badly blistered burn.

'You come through at once and I'll dress that for you,' she said. There was a murmur of assent from the people sitting there, and as Carmichael walked through with him a man remarked: 'They were wonderful, Sister. We owe them something today, I can tell you.'

The fireman looked slightly embarrassed and followed Carmichael through the plastic doors.

She took him, for privacy, into one of the now empty cubicles. He sat down heavily and took off his helmet revealing grey hair. He put it on the clean sheet on the bed, and then glanced hastily at Carmichael and said: 'Do you mind, Sister? I'm afraid it's a bit dirty.'

'Of course I don't mind,' said Carmichael and pushed the helmet further on to the disposable sheet and made him get up and take off his coat. He did so with some difficulty, so Carmichael helped him and hung it for him over the back of the chair. She rolled up his shirt sleeves and made him sit down

153

again with his arm resting on the disposable sheet. She decided
to do this dressing herself and fetched a small dressing tray. The
burn was not extensive, but he looked away as she got out a pair
of scissors and snipped round the burn, removed the skin and
dabbed the area dry as the serum ran out. Then she put on
cream and slipped a plastic glove over the top which would
protect the area and fastened it round his wrist.

'That's comfortable, Sister,' he said. 'They use these a lot
now, don't they, for hands and feet I mean?'

'Yes they do, these plastic bags help. You know dressings can
harm a burn quite a bit.' Carmichael spoke with authority.
Although she had not had a lot of experience with burns, this
night had taught her a great deal.

22

'I believe you've got one of our old mates here, haven't you? Derek Hanson. He's your fire officer now, isn't that right?'

Carmichael's heart lifted and began to beat faster at the very mention of Derek's name.

'Yes, we have. He was appointed some time ago and he's getting on very well here. I think he likes the job.' She was uncharacteristically verbose.

The firman leaned back and closed his eyes for a moment. He looked tired and Carmichael asked him if he would like a cup of tea. She went out to the waiting room where the WVS was installed and had been since the beginning of the disaster, making tea and coffee. These were some of the people who had to be summoned in the event of a major disaster and they had come willingly, quickly and had acted with great efficiency. They had been a help because they were well versed in the ways of hospitals and knew, for instance, that they mustn't give drinks to anyone who was having an anaesthetic.

Carmichael got a cup of tea and put two lumps of sugar in the saucer and took it back to the fireman. She put it beside him and he put out his good hand, taking it gratefully.

'Do you take sugar? There's some in the saucer,' Carmichael said almost primly and he looked up and smiled.

'Shock, eh? That's what you're thinking. I don't believe I am very shocked, I was at first but I don't think I am now. My hand hurt and I was going to go and let my wife dress it but I thought I'd better have it looked at. After all you never know, do you?'

Carmichael shook her head. 'You certainly don't. You were right to come along and have it dressed and you must come back tomorrow. We shall have to keep an eye on that, you've

155

lost quite a bit of skin there, you know.'

He nodded and looked at the hand encased in the plastic bag. 'Lucky to get away with just that, though,' he said. 'There were some terrible sights there, Sister – the ones that died. I reckon there were three but I can't be sure, we shall know tomorrow.'

'What caused the fire, do you know?' asked Carmichael. He shook his head.

'Electrical fault I should think, I'm not sure, though. It started in the basement somewhere. It was very quick. It was amazing really that there were so many people so quickly trapped. There was something inflammable down there. There's bound to be an inquiry. Anyway the foyer and hall were gutted in no time and that took in the staircase. I don't believe the emergency doors were easy to open. As I said, there's bound to be an inquiry, but what good will that do? The damage is done now.'

'That's why the hospital appointed the fire officer, I suppose. To check the emergency doors, fire-extinguishers, check that everything is always in order, that's why they appointed Derek . . .' She paused self consciously and then added his surname '. . . Hanson.'

He looked up at her over the rim of his teacup. 'That's right. Old Derek's not a bad chap. It's a good job for a fire chief to get, he was quite a good fire chief, bit of a one for the ladies, you know.' He winked at Carmichael. He was obviously feeling better, the tea was reviving him and Carmichael, who normally would have disliked the wink, smiled broadly.

'Yes, I believe he is,' she said. She was going to go on and confide in the man but something stopped her. She watched him sipping his tea in silence. Suddenly he smiled.

'Yes, I know his wife, know her well, I knew her as a girl.'

Carmichael felt herself freeze, become immobile, the sounds in the department receded from her and she felt curiously isolated as if she were alone somewhere with this man, alone and miles away. She pulled herself together. Of course he was wrong, it was ridiculous even to think of it.

'Oh no, I think you must be thinking of another Derek Hanson. Our fire officer is not married, he lost his wife, actually, in childbirth many years ago.'

156

The man looked up at her and put his now empty teacup down beside his helmet on the couch.

'No, Derek Hanson's married, he's got three kids. I've known them both for years and the kids too. They've never hit it off well. It's his fault, I can tell you that. She's quite a nice woman. Derek was a good fireman and a good fire chief and he'll make a fine hospital fire officer, but well, he's a bit weak with women – know what I mean?'

It was obvious that he was doing what so many people do – speaking frankly to a nurse, just because she was a nurse and used to receiving confidences. Carmichael had gone very white but the man didn't seem to notice.

'But they're divorced.' Carmichael made a statement of fact rather than asked a question.

The fireman shook his head. 'No, nothing like that. They're Catholics actually. They're not divorced, she wouldn't do that and I don't think he would really. No, they live sort of separate lives. They get together now and again and sometimes I think . . . and then well, he drifts off again, but that's Derek Hanson. Don't tell anyone I said it will you, Sister, I mean I shouldn't be talking like this.'

Carmichael turned and walked steadily out of the examination room. She needed quiet, somewhere to sit down. She felt things going black and misty around her as if she was going to faint as she walked towards her own office. Madeleine saw her and came forward quickly.

'Agnes, you look shocking. What on earth's the matter, has something . . .?'

'No, no, I'm all right.'

'Well, you've been working all day for goodness sake and it's getting into night now, it's after ten, you know. Don't you think you'd better go off duty?'

Carmichael looked around automatically. The place was now nearly empty, the atmosphere was still heavy with the stench of burning and smoke. She sat down in her office, quite still for a moment or two, her hands joined in her lap, loosely. She was relaxed and yet inside she was taut, it was a strange feeling. She couldn't really take in all the man had said, and yet his every word was engrained in her memory, as if it had been played on a tape recorder and she still had the tape and could play it again whenever she wished. Although she hadn't understood it the first time she had heard it, it was recorded carefully and accurately in her mind. She got to her feet and did one last round of the department, checking on the few patients who were left and having their dressings done.

Carmichael couldn't go without saying something to her nurses who were nearly all preparing to go off duty. She was conscious of Madeleine Taylor watching her, so she straightened her back and went up to the nurses and said: 'Thank you all for being so efficient and for staying on so late.'

The night nurses who had begun to take over looked surprised. Several of them who had worked for Carmichael for some time had never seen her in such a mellow mood.

Her nurses smiled uncertainly and said things like: 'Oh, it's all right, Sister,' or: 'We did our best and anyway you showed us what to do and we had that little lecture, you remember?'

They all seemed to have remembered that, Carmichael thought. She turned round to Madeleine Taylor.

'Good night, Sister Taylor and thank you. I'll try and make up some of the off duty during the week.'

Taylor waved her hand as if to say think nothing of it, but Carmichael insisted.

'Yes, I shall make it up to all of you. I'll work out exactly how many hours are owing to you and get out a new rota for next week.'

Carmichael knew she looked ill. She felt drained, but thank goodness her junior sister put it down, she could see, to tiredness and the strain of the day. Well, if she wanted to think that she could.

There was a noise of retreating footsteps and she looked up and saw the fireman making his way through the plastic doors. She had already told him she thought, or hoped, to report back tomorrow. That was all right. He had wrecked her life, but it was not his fault, he'd only been the messenger.

'Good night,' she said abruptly and walked out of the department, for once forgetting her cloak. She remembered it when she got to the door, went back to her office, picked up the cloak, slipped it round her shoulders and drew it firmly around her. She felt cold, very cold. She walked out of the department door, out of the front of the hospital and into the starry night. She would not think yet, she could not think yet. She must get home, shut herself in her room, a room that might be hers for the rest of her working life. Her thoughts were not registering properly because Derek Hanson and losing him would not come entirely into focus. She was thinking only of the long plod ahead until retirement.

There was a moon and it made strange shadows on the grass as she walked towards the nurses' home, strange, rectangular, black shadows on the path in front of her. She noticed them and registered them far more than anything else. This picture of the night seemed important. She got to the home door, pushed it open, stood for a moment as it swung heavily to behind her, then walked to her own room, put her key in the door, opened it and went inside. She threw off her cloak and sat down. Now, she supposed, was the time to think.

23

Next day was Carmichael's day off. She did all the usual things, had a bath, made up her face, and it was as she sat looking at herself in the mirror that she became aware of her own state of mind. She could not, or would not think. She was suddenly hit with the realization that, whether she admitted it or not, everything had altered. She had nothing, no future, no marriage, no man. It was all so different this morning and she could not take it in. One remark from a previously unknown man had shattered everything.

Then, as she sat there, she started wondering if the fireman could be wrong. Supposing Derek had had the marriage annulled and the fireman didn't know about it? Catholics did, she had seen it often in the papers and sometimes there were children involved too. It didn't seem to stop the marriage being annulled, the fact that there were children, if one of the pair wanted to get married again. She remembered reading of a case but couldn't recall whether one had been a Catholic and the other Protestant. Neither could she be sure what the fireman had said. Had he said that the wife had been a Catholic and Derek was not? She could not remember Derek Hanson ever mentioning religious beliefs. Hope stirred, only to be dashed the next minute by recollecting what he had said when they had been out to dinner that first evening, about his wife dying in childbirth. That of course must have been a lie. And yet . . .? No wait, could it have been true? When he was very young could he have married and had a young wife who . . .? She rose and wandered about the room, her mind switching from hope to despair. When she had finished dressing she felt she must get out. She couldn't bear her thoughts, she couldn't put up with any more doubt. Suddenly, just as she was putting on her coat, there was a knock on her door and her heart lifted. Was it Derek? Had he come to see her to ask about last night? When she told him of his colleague's disclosures perhaps he would be able to put everything right. But no, it was a nurse who poked her head round the door and said: 'You're wanted on the telephone, Sister.'

Carmichael thanked her and the nurse disappeared. She heard her running along the corridor and then taking the stairs two at a time and she thought: how lovely to be as young as that.

She made her way out of her room and along to the telephone in the hall. She picked up the receiver, it was Derek.

'What a day you had yesterday, Agnes!' he said, his voice full of sympathy. 'I didn't come round to the home, I heard you were still on duty at ten, but I'd like to take you out tonight. I can be off at six or half past easily if that's all right with you. We'll go out to dinner and it will help take your mind off that awful day you must have had. Is that all right?'

Carmichael could hardly speak. She just managed to say: 'Yes,' and then had to clear her throat and repeat the word. 'Yes, Derek,' she said. She had to see him, she had to talk to him, she had to know. 'Yes, that will be all right. I'll be ready.'

Derek sounded cheerful and his usual self, but then why shouldn't he? He didn't know that she . . .

'Great, I'm so looking forward to seeing you, Agnes,' he went on. 'As I said, I didn't ring you last night, I thought you'd be so tired after all that had gone on. I went to the department this morning. I forgot it was your day off, but Sister Taylor told me. See you tonight then.'

'Yes, Derek, yes, I'll look forward to that.'

Carmichael tried to sound like her usual self but it was difficult. As she turned away from the phone she felt suddenly dizzy and realized that she had not had any breakfast and no proper supper last night. As far as she could remember she hadn't eaten since yesterday lunchtime. She must have something. The very thought of food made her feel physically sick. She would make herself some coffee. She went back to her room and collected a jar of instant coffee and some powered milk and made her way towards the kitchen. As she went in she was greeted by Sister O'Hara. She was still in her dressing-gown and her red curls were in a riot round her head, her ample bosom was slightly exposed by the dressing-gown which was hanging open.

'Hallo, we meet again, do we? History repeating itself.' At Carmichael's blank look she continued: 'You remember, we met here in the kitchen one evening, didn't we? At least I think it was in the evening but frankly I can't remember whether it was night or morning but I know we met.'

Carmichael did not feel like speaking to her or anyone else and she inclined her head.

O'Hara with her usual open, generous, extrovert manner which Carmichael had envied when she met her in the kitchen before continued: 'There's some milk over, do you want it or are you going to make coffee? I'll leave it on the stove for you if you like, it's hot, I've just made mine! A cup of coffee was on the kitchen table, steaming, and beside it a plate of buttered toast. O'Hara moved the wooden chair away from the table and sat down, pulling the chair with a rasping noise closer to the table again. She picked up a piece of toast and sank her white teeth in it, the butter bubbling out over her full, red lips. She pulled the toast away, munched a little, then looked at Carmichael again.

'You had a bit of a time in Casualty yesterday, didn't you?' Some of them were warded, weren't they? We didn't get any, thank goodness, but I heard two of them were admitted during the night.'

Carmichael knew all this, but it didn't seem to affect her, she thought dully. But then she felt her mind was dull, like blotting paper. She had to say something to O'Hara so she finished pouring the hot milk on her coffee, stirred it and thanked her.

'Piece of toast?' O'Hara pushed the plate towards her but Carmichael shook her head and attempted to sip the coffee which was too hot.

'It's my day off today, but I shall go on duty, I shall go on and do the rota to make up the off duty that the nurses lost, I feel I should do that.'

It was an unnecessary remark, but Carmichael had the feeling that she must say something to this woman sitting so comfortably there beside the kitchen table, just as if she were in her own home. Carmichael felt a longing to go over and be clasped in O'Hara's rather fat arms, put her head on the ample bosom and tell her everything and cry and cry and cry. But that was something Carmichael could never do and she knew it.

Instead she said stiffly: 'Well, I must take this back to my room. I was writing a letter.'

'I wouldn't go on duty if I were you, you've got your junior sister, who is it . . . Taylor isn't it? She could do the rota for you, couldn't she? Give her a ring and tell her to do it. I'm blowed if I'd go on when you had such a rough day yesterday. You look all in.'

'I must. I must go and see everything is all right,' said Carmichael and was about to leave when O'Hara said something which arrested her.

'Oh, by the way, did you hear the result of the autopsy on poor old Pearson?'

Carmichael raised her head and looked directly at O'Hara.

'No, no, I haven't heard it. What did it say?'

'Death by strangulation. Well, we all knew that, didn't we? Somehow, I thought she might be pregnant. You know what a silly little bitch Debbie was. She might have forgotten to take the pill or she might have stopped taking it deliberately to catch someone. Maybe that was who killed her. But she wasn't preg. I never believed in the flasher somehow, I think it was someone else. I believe the flasher it there all right, but I don't think they murder, do they, not flashers, not from what I've heard anyway.'

Carmichael was hardly listening to the latter part of O'Hara's chatter, though she did make some reply that seemed to satisfy the woman. She made for the door, carrying the coffee carefully so as not to spill it, and was careful, too, not to turn quickly in case the dizziness that she had felt when she had left the telephone returned.

'Thanks for the milk,' she said again, 'I must go back to my room, I must finish that letter.'

'Yes, I should go back to your room and have a rest. We're not as young as we were you know.' O'Hara gave a low, rich, throaty laugh and for once Carmichael did not care about the reference to age. It seemed pointless now to worry about it. She walked back to her room.

It was twelve o'clock when Carmichael walked into the Casualty department in uniform. Madeleine Taylor was obviously surprised to see her.

'Hey, what are you doing on duty? I thought it was your day off, and from the way you looked last night I would have said you could do with it. You look pretty pale this morning.'

This irritated Carmichael and it must have shown for Madeleine Taylor said hastily: 'Sorry, it's nothing to do with me, it's not my business if you want to come on duty.'

'I just felt that I would like to do the rota, to pay the nurses back for the extra hours they put in yesterday. I thought I would rather do it at once, I think Miss Thompson will expect it.' Carmichael walked into her office and the junior sister followed her.

'Anything else the matter, Agnes?'

The irritation that Carmichael felt increased. She was aware that now her life with a man and her future was in jeopardy. The nice, benign, comfortable feeling towards Madeleine Taylor and Nigel Denton was waning. She tried to stem a feeling almost of dislike for the girl in front of her.

'Do you want me to help you?' Sister Taylor hovered a little, sensitive enough, Carmichael thought, to register the feeling of animosity that Carmichael knew she was giving out.

'No, no, thank you. I can do it myself perfectly well,' she said more sharply than she had intended and Taylor beat a hasty retreat. Carmichael saw the slight grimace on her face and also saw that her cheeks had reddened. Madeleine Taylor blushed easily. This was probably one of the things Nigel Denton and other men found attractive, thought Carmichael bitterly.

After she had finished doing the new rota she beckoned her junior sister to come back to the office.

'There you are, Sister Taylor, I've finished it. I've scattered the extra hours to repay them over the week. You can tell them, if you will.'

'Right, thanks. We've been pretty slack this morning.' She obviously was trying not to offend.

164

'Oh yes,' said Carmichael, showing very little interest and Madeleine Taylor spoke again.

'Oh, by the way, Derek Hanson came. He'd forgotten it was your day off and I told him you would probably be in the nurses' home and he said he'd ring you. Was that all right?'

'Yes, yes, thank you, he did telephone me,' said Carmichael and got up to go but Taylor had something else to tell her.

'Oh, the autopsy on Debbie Pearson – death by strangulation – that's about all, all that I've heard anyway.'

'Yes, I know. Sister O'Hara told me, I met her in the kitchen this morning.'

'Oh, Sister O'Hara, she knows everything before anyone else, nice woman though, I like her. I'm going to ask her to my wedding. I met her when I was a junior. She was awfully kind to me and I'll never forget it.'

Carmichael turned away abruptly. She didn't want to hear anything about Madeleine Taylor's wedding, anything at all.

'Well, I think I'll go back to the home now, you won't want me. You're fully staffed this afternoon and this evening.'

'Yes we are. It was good of you to come and do the extra duty rota. I'd forgotten it, though I expect the nurses would have reminded me, sure thing. Are you going to have some lunch? I can come with you if you like.' She looked at her watch. 'It's nearly half past twelve.'

'No, I don't think so, thank you. I think I'll go back to the home.'

'Have you had any breakfast, Agnes?'

Although she would have liked to, Carmichael felt she couldn't show irritation at this remark. Madeleine Taylor's voice was warm and kind, and sounded really anxious.

'No, I haven't. I just couldn't eat any, I must be off my food. I've had some coffee though.'

'Well, why don't you go back to the home and go to bed, have a snooze, fill a hot water bottle and snuggle down in bed. You'll feel better after you've had a sleep. Did you have a good night?'

Carmichael felt this to be too much of an intrusion on her privacy, she'd had enough. She did not want to talk to Madeleine Taylor about how she had slept, what she had eaten

165

or how she felt. She said coldly: 'Yes, I did thank you, I had a very good night and if I feel like having some lunch I'll go into the town and get some.'

She walked out of her office grabbing her cloak as she did so and swinging it round her. She could see that Taylor obviously felt that she had been dismissed. She said no more and Carmichael walked out of the department speaking to some of her nurses as they greeted her.

As Carmichael made her way back to the home to change out of her uniform she thought of the rest of the day in front of her. Suddenly she made a resolve, she knew exactly what she would do to make herself feel better. She would ring up the beautician and make an appointment to have her hair done and perhaps also have a facial and have her face made-up. She was bound to be able to get in if she didn't insist on her usual assistant. Yes, that's what she would do – she would make herself look exactly as she had that day when she had come out of the beautician's and bumped into Derek. Yes, that's what she would do. She had got to face him tonight and she was determined to face him looking her best.

This decision made her feel better and as she walked to the home and then through the doors she remembered the passbook in her handbag, the passbook that she had not yet used to get the two thousand pounds that Derek Hanson wanted. Well, that in a way was a good thing, she supposed, but it was a bleak good thing, for she knew that she would gladly give him that two thousand pounds if only – if only he were going to be her husband. Maybe he still would, maybe there was still a little hope. That fireman in Casualty had perhaps been wrong. On that she was building her hopes.

She walked with a firmer step towards her room, then turned, remembering Antoinette's, and dialled the beautician's number.

24

Carmichael was wearing a dress she knew Derek liked and she was conscious of the fact that her hair and face, so recently done at Antoinette's, were in immaculate order and that she was looking her best. A touch of her perfume and she was ready.

Her appearance gave her confidence. Although she was dreading the evening, she was still cherishing the hope that Derek might be able to put everything right, to allay her fears, explain.

As his car drew up outside the sun was still shining, which for some reason added to her feeling of confidence. She opened the door of the home and went out to the car. Derek, as usual, leapt out and went round to the passenger's side to let her in. She stood there for a second looking at him. He kissed her quickly, on the cheek, looking round first because he knew that she didn't like any outward show of affection if anyone was watching. Tonight though he got no answering smile.

She got into the car and did up her seat belt while he went round to the driver's side. Carmichael wondered if this would be the last time she would go out with him, because if she faced him this evening with the fact that she had heard he was married and he couldn't convince her otherwise, that, she was determined, would be the end of it. The end of these lovely drives, the end of going to some nice wayside pub for that intimate drink, of those walks, of those dinners and picnics.

'You're very quiet, Agnes,' he said as he started the car.

She turned to him, looked at him directly and said: 'Yes, I believe I'm a little bit tired after yesterday.'

'You don't look it, you look absolutely wonderful,' said Derek and turned his eyes back to the road.

Carmichael felt her neck redden with pleasure as it always did, never her cheeks. Had it all been worth it? If this relationship was to end, then, it hadn't – for she had built the relationship in the hope of permanence.

'Where are we going?' she asked.

'I thought I'd take you to Swallows. It's a new place, about fifteen miles away but we've plenty of time. It's by the river and everyone seems to be talking about it. I thought you'd like to try it. I haven't been there.'

'Yes, I would.' Carmichael was silent again and did not speak to him again for some miles. As they drove along the country road she could feel Derek casting curious glances at her every so often, but she felt here, in the car, she could say nothing.

He tried to start the conversation again.

'You must have had a terribly busy day yesterday, that fire was pretty awful, so I hear. I haven't seen the site but . . .'

'I have,' said Carmichael and indeed she had. When she had gone to the beauty parlour that afternoon she had seen the devastation at the hotel opposite.

'It's a wonder, from what I hear, that there were not more people hurt,' said Derek.

'Two died, two were admitted to the ward and I hear they died,' said Carmichael. Her tone was flat, without animation, and again she could feel the man beside her looking at her curiously.

'You mustn't worry about it, Agnes. You did your best, I'm sure, and I know how well you treat everyone. You sound dreadfully depressed,' Derek said and Carmichael nodded.

'Yes, I suppose it was rather a depressing evening, there were some bad burns. We were able to treat quite a few and I'm sure they'll be all right. There were one or two firemen too.'

She glanced at him sideways, she could see only his profile and that expressed nothing, and she knew that he did not even suspect that she had met someone who knew him, someone who had told her he was a married man with three children. But then the fireman had been grey-haired and perhaps the only one who knew Derek well. Carmichael began to feel slightly sick again. She couldn't cope with it yet, she couldn't speak about it to him here in the car, she would have to wait.

She sat up straighter and tried to enjoy the evening drive. After all, if it was to be the last she would have with Derek, it would be stupid to spoil it. She could wait till they got to Swallows, wherever that was, then face him with it. She experienced a horrible clutching feeling in the pit of her stomach as she thought of it, and she wished for a moment that she had some tranquillizers left over from the time long ago when she had had to take them. However, she was determined not to become addicted to tranquillizers again, so whatever happened she would have to endure it without help. She'd got her job, she'd have to continue with it. But the feeling of sickness and the clutching feeling did not go away, and she did not enjoy the drive.

As they neared the river Derek Hanson remarked: 'It's along here somewhere. There's a lawn in front stretching down to the river. I don't know it it's warm enough to sit out there. If it isn't we can sit inside. I believe it's very pretty. Here it is.'

He slowed the car and turned to the left into the car-park that already had one or two cars in it although it was still early. It certainly was an attractive place, a long, low building, which looked as if several cottages had been converted into one. On each side of the house the river stretched away. There were willows on the bank, their new leaves swaying in the very slight, warm breeze and the ends of their branches just touching the water. It was like a picture postcard and Carmichael wished, oh how she wished, that this was one of their normal evenings, that she had learned nothing about a wife and children, that she knew nothing about his affairs or anything, that they were just a man and a woman going out for an evening before their engagement was announced. What a lovely place this was, what a lovely place if he were about to propose to her. But if that man in Casualty last night had been right how could he?

They walked through the low front door into Swallows and found themselves in a prettily decorated hall. They made their way through into the bar which was almost empty. Two men at one end talked quietly. A white-coated barman was polishing a glass and gazing into the distance. He brightened up as they came in.

'Good evening, sir, madam.'

Derek walked towards the door leading out on to the lawn and Carmichael followed him. There were chairs and tables standing on the patio, but they were empty. They both stood there for a moment, gazing at the river. It made a slight rippling noise as it flowed by and little tiny white-topped wavelets lapped the shore where celandines were blooming.

'This is really something isn't it, Agnes? What a lovely place. It's strange, isn't it, that being by water is always attractive.'

'Yes, yes it is. I love the river and the sea,' said Carmichael, but she thought to herself that she had every reason to hate rivers for once she had nearly drowned herself in one and once she had drowned someone else. She turned away abruptly and went back indoors and sat down at a table as far away from the bar as she could get. She wanted to talk and she did not want the barman to overhear. She could not eat her dinner unless he knew what she had heard, had, perhaps, managed to reassure her that it was not the truth.

He said again: 'What's the matter, Agnes? I still think you're suffering from yesterday. You're too sensitive. What would you like to drink, the usual?'

She nodded dumbly, brandy was as good as anything else, she thought. She was becoming rather a brandy drinker since she had been going out with Derek, but it didn't matter. She might need the brandy and so might Derek.

When he went to the bar she thought to herself, one of the things in Derek's favour is that he's not mean; then she thought again of the two hundred pounds he'd borrowed from Pearson, according to what she had heard, and of the two thousand he was hoping to borrow from her. Perhaps that was why he had no need to be mean. For the moment she put that thought out of her mind and waited passively for him to come back with the drinks.

'Would you like to go outside? I think it's warm enough, you've got your coat on.'

Carmichael looked up at him.

'Yes, yes perhaps it would be nice.' She thought that perhaps more people would come into the bar and perhaps it would be better outside by the river, in the open air. She felt she might be able to talk more freely and so might he. She rose and they walked through the door they had already been through, and sat down outside. Carmichael half regretted her decision, for the breeze was slightly chilly and the wrought iron of the chair hurt her back, making her lean forward a little.

Derek put the glasses down and, drawing a deep breath of satisfaction, said: 'Lovely, lovely after having been in the hospital all day, isn't it?'

Carmichael felt he was trying very hard to be agreeable, to get her out of her depression and of course this was nice of him, she recognized that. It was thoughtful of him to try and cheer her up, believing that she was depressed after seeing all the burns, the horrors of yesterday. She looked at him. The sunlight was glinting on his wavy hair and his skin looked particularly clear and brown. She longed to touch his face, she longed to have him kiss her passionately and have everything she had heard from the fireman disproved. She longed to hear him say: 'Oh Agnes, how silly of you to doubt me, of course I'm not married, that was annulled years ago. She was very difficult, my wife, and she's living with another man. Anyway there's nothing to it, don't worry.'

Suddenly Carmichael felt she could wait no longer. Almost in the middle of something Derek was saying, she said abruptly: 'Derek, I have to ask you. Yesterday evening in Casualty I treated a fireman named Best. He said he was a friend of yours and that you have a wife. He told me you have three children.'

There was a long silence. Her eyes looked at him begging for denial, begging for him to say anything that would enable their life together to go on, anything that would make her safe, make her safe with him for the rest of her life.

25

The silence seemed to go on and on for ever and the noise of the river seemed, in Carmichael's mind, to fill it with ugly slapping noises that before were so pleasant. Derek slumped in his chair looking older. He looked out over the water and Carmichael waited, but his very silence warned her of what he was going to say.

'Yes, Agnes, he was right. I've known Best for years. He knows Adelaide, my wife, and the kids. Yes, I'm married, it's just one of those things, I don't know. We live apart most of the time, go our own way, we just don't get on. When I'm at home we row all the time. I go and see her of course and stay for a bit. Well, it's that that makes me short of money as you can imagine. Not that that was why I wanted to borrow the money from you, it was, as I said, for a friend.' He would not meet her eyes and Carmichael knew that he was lying about that too.

'Why didn't you tell me all this before?' Carmichael asked.

'I enjoy your company and I knew, I knew you weren't the kind of . . . well, you wouldn't like it, would you, going out with a married man? A married man with three kids. You see you're the kind of woman I could live with and be happy with for the rest of my life, Agnes.'

'And what about the others?' Carmichael felt she was twisting the knife in her wound, not his. 'What about Debbie Pearson? What about the girl who was so bitter against you, the one on the surgical ward, the one who you say was blackmailing you, have you had an affair with her too? Is that why she's so bitter?'

'I'm not a saint, I never have been, Agnes.'

Carmichael felt empty, as if everything had been taken away

172

from her in one grasp by some terrible hand of fate. The whole life that had stretched before her had gone. She was alone again, she knew it.

'Why, why me?' she asked. 'I'm not young, I'm not . . .' – she hesitated to use the word – '. . . sexy, like either of those girls. Why me?'

'Because I found you to be a very nice companion. As I said, I like being with you, our times together were pleasant. I've grown very fond of you, Agnes.'

Carmichael's bitter smile did not go away. She realized he couldn't say: 'Look, I never promised you anything, what are you moaning about?' He had to stay pleasant, flattering, he still entertained faint hopes of the two thousand pounds, but most of all because of the alibi. Derek noticed her smile.

'What are you smiling at?' he asked. 'You'll still stand by me, won't you? I mean I can't expect you to lend me the money if you don't trust me, but you'll still back me up about that evening, won't you? I had nothing to do with Debbie's death, nothing whatever.'

'Didn't you, Derek?' Carmichael looked at him. Any feeling she had for him was turning sour – curdling in the chill evening breeze. She got up.

'Let's go and have another drink,' she said, 'but we'll have it inside, it's getting cold out here.'

They walked in, she was shattered, but she knew she was buoyed up by hate. She still had the whip hand over him and for the moment she would use it.

She sat down in a more comfortable seat away from the bar. She ran her hand over the red upholstery. She was still smiling a little. She hurt, oh yes, she hurt, but she still had power.

Derek came back with further drinks and put them down. As he did so he looked at her and it was obvious to Carmichael that he could not understand her mood. She did not return his glance but she felt his eyes continue to look at her as he sat down next to her on the red upholstered seat. He put his hand out and covered hers as he had done so many times. She did not take her hand away, she kept it there, inert. He squeezed her hand but she did not react to that.

'Can't we . . . can't we go on like this, as we are? Does it

173

make a difference to you the fact that I've got a wife and children? I mean it is the 1980s, and we're not . . .'

Carmichael raised her eyes to his.

'Yes, it does make a difference. I thought quite differently from you. I thought we might spend the rest of our lives together, retire together. Stupid of me, wasn't it?'

He stammered then: 'I-I never said, I-I never gave you . . .'

'No, you didn't, it was me. I had those thoughts, not you. We can't go on. I don't want to go out with a married man who has affairs with nasty little women like Debbie Pearson and, I suspect, with the other girl too, probably with many more. I suppose she holds me against you, that girl on the surgical ward, and the fact that you're going out with me, is that it?'

Derek shook his head, but he did not deny anything and Carmichael knew she was probably right. She sipped her drink, gazing ahead of her, and waited. She knew he would say something about the winning cards she held in her hand so firmly.

'You won't . . . I know how you feel about the money if you don't want to lend it to me now I shall quite understand.'

'I don't,' said Carmichael calmly. Inside she felt she was crying, but outside she felt cold.

'Well, that's perfectly all right, but if Inspector Murphy says anything you will still say that I was with you, won't you? You won't go back on that, will you? I know I've behaved badly but I didn't kill Debbie Pearson and if you tell them . . . you will, won't you? I mean, how would I explain where I was, if I said I was with her it would . . . you will back me up and say I was with you, from quarter past eight, you will won't you?'

There was real fear in his eyes now and Carmichael wondered just how deeply he was in trouble with the inspector. Well, it was his problem now. She finished her drink and got up.

'You can take me home now, Derek,' she said. 'I feel rather tired. It's probably, as you say, a reaction from yesterday and from everything else.'

'But you will, you will bear me out in that, won't you? It's terribly important. I feel they think I was Debbie's boyfriend. Suppose they found out I was with her that night?'

'Well you were, weren't you? And she did tell you she was

174

pregnant, didn't she?'

'How do you know that?' Derek's eyes were round with astonishment.

'I guessed. I know that kind of woman,' said Carmichael calmly. She walked out of the doorway, back into the car-park, and he followed her. She stood there patiently with her hand on the car door waiting for it to be unlocked. He snapped the lock and she got in.

They drove back to the nurses' home in complete silence and when they arrived she did not look at him, but immediately prepared to get out of the car. He jumped out and came and opened the door for her, his eyes fixed on hers anxiously. Carmichael knew that she was completely in charge of the situation and her heart was heavy, very heavy.

'You won't . . . you won't . . . forget, will you, Agnes,' and he put his hand on hers, but she drew back.

'Good night, Derek, and thank you for the drinks,' she said and walked round the car into the nurses' home, feeling his eyes watching her.

Back in her room she sat down. Everything was gone, everything. She gazed in her mirror: her make-up had stood up well, so had her hair. Everything about her looked quite attractive, she thought. But it was useless, useless. No more dates, no more quiet secluded dinners, never again to feel his warm hand on hers. She put her head down between her hands and the tears came between her fingers, ruining her make-up she thought. She did not care, hate welled up again to help her – hate, loathing of this man who had given her a false sense of security, a false sense of belonging, a false sense of loving. He was nothing. He was just a womanizer who tried to get money out of everyone, every woman he met. For a moment she regretted what she had done to Pearson. After all, she was about what Derek Hanson deserved. Still, it was done and she didn't really regret it, the patients would be better off without a nurse like that around. Hatred, the old hatred came back to sustain her. She got up, washed the make-up off her face and viciously combed the set out of her hair. What did it matter? What did she matter? What did her looks matter? Nothing. She would take up her life again as best she could. As for Derek, he

175

would eventually wish he had never met her. As well as the raging hate that seemed to possses her, Carmichael was filled with a terrible desolation.

26

It was eleven o'clock the following day when Carmichael was once again summoned to the police incident room. Sister Taylor was off duty so Carmichael told her senior staff nurse that she was temporarily having to leave the department. She was thankful that they were not too busy this morning, but she was also well aware that Casualty could have a sudden influx of patients with various ailments, one after the other. A seemingly slack morning could turn into a hectic one.

'I'll try not to be long. I'm going to see Inspector Murphy, he wants to ask me some more questions about Nurse Pearson. If anything urgent comes up do not hesitate to send for me.'

'I will, Sister,' Staff Nurse Burton answered.

As Carmichael drew near the incident room – they had taken over the resident doctors' rest room and the doctors were housed for the moment in the consultants' room – the door opened and, as had happened before, she met Derek Hanson coming out. He looked, she thought, white and harassed, but Carmichael could not read the expression on his face. When she saw her, when his eyes met hers, once again there was that pleading in them, begging her to do as he had asked, say he was with her that fateful evening. He closed the door behind him and was obviously trying to snatch a chance to speak to her but she passed him avoiding his eyes and opened the door herself even though his hand came out to do so. After tapping lightly on the panel and hearing the Inspector's soft Irish voice say 'Enter,' she went in shutting the door firmly behind her, almost in Derek's face. She felt as she did so that she was shutting him out of her life for ever.

Inspector Murphy looked up as she came forward and rose to

177

his feet politely, motioning to the chair opposite to his desk.

'Please sit down, Sister Carmichael,' he said. 'There are just one or two small points I would like to go over with you.'

'Certainly, Inspector, but I am rather busy this morning.'

'Of course, I quite understand, I will not keep you a moment longer than is absolutely necessary. I do know how busy you sisters are.' He looked down at the notes on his desk and then sat down.

Carmichael, seated opposite him, had her hands in her lap and her back straight.

'We can assume that Miss Pearson died approximately around nine o'clock, or slightly before. This is based on the pathologist's report and of course on the fact that the deceased girl would hardly have stayed out in the open to meet her boyfriend, or whoever it was she was meeting, during the thunderstorm, which started at nine o'clock if you remember?'

Carmichael could remember only too well and as she sat there opposite the inspector she almost felt again the first heavy thunder drops on her skin.

'Yes, I do remember,' she said.

'We feel that Nurse Pearson was strangled before the storm had started, Sister Carmichael,' the police inspector continued.

'You say that you saw her leave your Casualty department at eight thirty, so it would seem that that half hour before the onset of the storm may well have been the time of the murder. What I wish to ascertain is this. I feel there must have been some struggle but you have said you heard nothing although your room is not a long way from where she was murdered.'

'I heard nothing at all,' Carmichael said calmly.

The inspector nodded his head slowly and Carmichael noticed that he had drawn a small circle on the blotting paper in front of him and was slowly filling it in with his pen.

'Did you know that your friend, Mr Hanson, knew the deceased woman intimately?' he asked, suddenly looking up.

Carmichael looked down at her hands, thinking: so the nurse on women's surgical had talked and Derek would need her alibi more than ever. Carmichael's mouth twisted into her downward smile.

'Yes, I know that,' she answered lightly. 'He told me that he knew the girl fairly intimately but they had parted company before he came to the hospital, that's what he told me.' Carmichael watched the inspector resume filling in the small circle on his blotting paper.

'It seems strange you heard nothing of a struggle, but of course, as you have already said, your window was closed.'

'That is correct. I dislike closing my window in the summer but those of us who live on the ground floor have been told to keep our windows closed by the police. It's because of the prowler – the flasher as they call him.'

Again the inspector nodded his slow nod and Carmichael waited, her hands clasped in her lap. Now, she thought, now would come the question for which she was waiting, she felt sure of it. However, the form it took rather startled her.

'And of course you were talking, were you not, and that would make it more unlikely that you would hear anything.'

She felt the inspector's eyes fixed on her face. He had left the little circle now, put the pen down, clasped his hands on the desk and was looking at her intently.

'Talking? No, I was alone, to whom would I be talking?' Carmichael asked.

Inspector Murphy frowned. 'But Mr Hanson tells me he was with you. He called for you at eight thirty after a meeting in the hospital.'

There was a long pause.

Carmichael affected a bewildered surprise. 'Oh no,' she said, almost demurely. 'Mr Hanson must be making a mistake, he did not call for me until quarter to ten. I know the time because he remarked on it. He said he had been kept late at the meeting and apologized to me. In fact, he said we would just have time to motor out somewhere for a drink.'

'I see.' Inspector Murphy had started another circle on the blotting pad, then again he abruptly stopped his doodling.

'Sister Carmichael, it might be necessary for you to repeat that statement at a later date. I would like you to be sure that it is quite correct.'

'Certainly I would repeat it if it became necessary,' Carmichael replied quietly, but positively. 'I know this is a very serious matter, a nurse has been killed, murdered, and the truth

179

must be adhered to. But why . . .'

Inspector Murphy did not reply to her implied question.

'Thank you, Sister Carmichael. That is really all I have to ask. I don't think I need to detain you any longer. Thank you for being so helpful.'

Carmichael wondered if she was imagining it, or did the inspector look at her rather strangely? She wondered too how much had been said to Derek Hanson, what had made him look so white, so harassed as he had met her outside the door. Oh well . . .

Carmichael rose to her feet, hesitated a moment, then walked to the door, but there she turned.

'Inspector Murphy, where will it . . . when will you want me . . .?'

'Not yet, Sister Carmichael, not yet, but in the rather near future I imagine you might be asked that question again. Try not to worry. It is always an ordeal if you know the person concerned.'

Although Carmichael felt a strange screaming inside her head – high and piercing – splitting her in half as if something was being torn alive out of her life, nevertheless she answered composedly: 'Not at all, Inspector. I shall be only too pleased.'

QUARTET  QRIME

MEL ARRIGHI
Alter Ego

MEG ELIZABETH ATKINS
Palimpsest

DAVID CARKEET
Double Negative

ANTHEA COHEN
Angel Without Mercy
Angel of Vengeance
Angel of Death
Fallen Angel
Guardian Angel
Hell's Angel

RUTH DUDLEY EDWARDS
Corridors of Death
The St Valentine's Day Murders

SHIRLEY ESKAPA
Blood Fugue

DAVID E. FISHER
The Man You Sleep With
Variation on a Theme

ALAN FURST
The Paris Drop
The Caribbean Account
Shadow Trade

JOHN GREENWOOD
Murder, Mr Mosley
Mosley by Moonlight
Mosley Went to Mow

ELLA GRIFFITHS
Murder on Page Three

183

RAY HARRISON
French Ordinary Murder
Death of an Honourable Member
Deathwatch
Death of a Dancing Lady

MICHAEL HATFIELD
Spy Fever

JOHN HAYTHORNE
The Strelsau Dimension

PETER LEVI
Grave Witness

J.C.S. SMITH
Nightcap

GUNNAR STAALESEN
At Night All Wolves Are Grey

LEONARD TOURNEY
Low Treason
Familiar Spirits